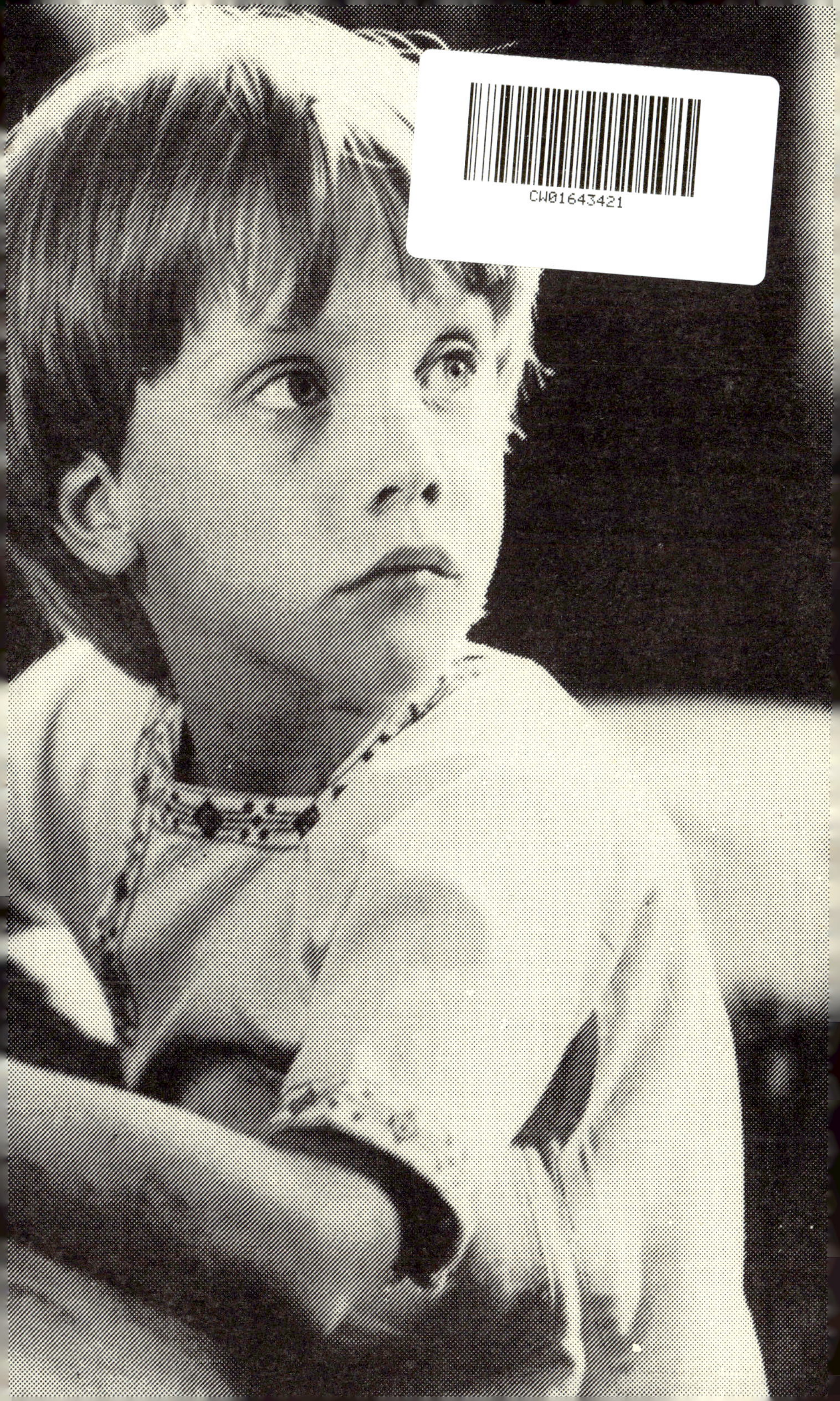

THE ENCHANTED WAY

BY THE SAME AUTHOR

THE YEAR OF THE BULL

OSCAR PARLAND

THE ENCHANTED WAY

TRANSLATED
FROM THE SWEDISH
BY JOAN TATE

PETER OWEN
LONDON & CHESTER SPRINGS PA

To Heidi

PETER OWEN PUBLISHERS
73 Kenway Road London SW5 0RE
Peter Owen books are distributed in the USA by
Dufour Editions Inc. Chester Springs PA 19425-0449

Translated from the Swedish *Den förtrollade vägen*

First published in Great Britain 1991

British Library Cataloguing in Publication Data
Parland, Oscar *1912*–
The enchanted way.
I. Title
839.7374 [F]

ISBN 0-7206-0829-5

Typeset in Melior by Action Typsetting Limited Gloucester
Printed in Great Britain by Billings of Worcester

The endpapers show a scene from *Lumotto tie* (The Enchanted Way) (courtesy of Yleisradio, Finnish Broadcasting Company)

Preface

> If you travel every path you will not find the limits of the soul, so deep is its account.
>
> HERACLITUS

THE ORIGINS OF THE SOUL ARE MYTHICAL. PAST knowledge of mankind and the individual is a story with no beginning. As I look back through the paths of memory in search of my origins, I always come to a point where I no longer know which direction to take and am overcome with confusion at having lost my way, no longer able to distinguish between memory, poetry and fantasy. Proportions have changed and meanings shifted; things are no longer what they would appear to be, everything so much more ambiguous, more enigmatic than in the world I inhabit today.

As in the myth, I am surrounded by supernatural semi-divine, semi-animal creatures. The animals speak with human tongues – all is an incarnation of the Soul, which shapes the material according to its own laws and gives it life and face. The omnipotence of the Soul is infinite, like that of Our Lord as he hovered over the water and created the world from nothing. Every object on which the eye dwells is lit from within and transformed into a mirror reflecting the image of the Soul. After that it lives its own life, marked and shaped by the Soul.

1

THE TWILIGHT THAT EVENING WAS GREY AND VIOLET, A faintly metallic twilight, as when you blow on a pocket mirror and see your face quickly and mysteriously darken. Soft as cotton wool, it gives you a rare sense of well-being mixed with delirium.

In this twilight, I am flying along the avenue of birches together with Bernt. Oh, how quickly we're flying! The tree-trunks rise and fall flat behind us and the blackness of the fencing blinks. Bernt's skis squeak and his ski-sticks creak each time he pulls the points out of the icy crust of snow in order to fling them forward. Only the moon can keep up, the moon a honey-yellow drop of light bowling along in the black network of birch branches, winking at us. Then our shadows, thin, silent friends flapping and dancing jerkily along the edge of the road.

Why does the moon follow us? Why does he run? What is he looking for? He usually follows me, silently and stubbornly like a stray cat. I never notice it unless I pay special attention. Sometimes he goes down into a forest or behind a house, but after a while he comes creeping round behind the corner of the house or in a tree-top. He has been following me all the time in the forest or behind the wall of the house. All three of us are now running together again.

The avenue comes to an end and we have arrived at the Black Gateway, the two halves of the gate like the ends of Grandmother's bed. The field sloping down towards the lake is quite close, surrounded by tall, dark spruces, and it is nearly always chilly and damp there. We plunge into a dark vault, the moon and the shadows suddenly gone. In the silence, we can hear the rippling of the melting snow and my boots splashing in water. The road is quite black, covered with horse-droppings and ice. Bernt's skis won't slide any more.

We go on slowly, here and there stepping over pale-blue patches of moonlight. In places, the road is iced right over, as if covered with glass, and on the dark patches spreading out round the trees we can see how much snow has melted since the day before, and the way the bare ground, with its tufts of moss, bilberry scrub and pine-needles, captures new territory every day. Spring transforms everything, melting the snow into glass and crystallized fruit, pricking holes through the crust of snow under the trees like a strainer and drawing winding veins of water in the icy armour of the roads.

The road now curves and we come to the slope up to Uncle Georg's, our steps growing slower and slower the higher we go, the snow there melted in places and our feet sinking into the bare earth. It feels soft and alive, the swiftly running water glinting like plaited glass in ruts.

When we finally reach the top of the hill, I turn round to look for the moon, and he has got behind after all, now right behind us, high up above the spruce tops by the Black Gateway. He is so far away, it's difficult to see properly what he is like. I can see he is quite round, shiny and glistening, hanging up there in the pale-violet arch of the sky like a plate of gold. The Old Man in the Moon lives on his gleaming surface. You can probably see him, though not as clearly as you see the moon himself. He is shadowy, as if he were a cobweb, but I can see he resembles Uncle Georg. This is Uncle Georg's hill, so he can see us and he listens to us, although he is invisible and isn't there himself. Uncle Georg wears glasses and has a moon-gleaming beard, and actually he is the one who is the Old Man in the Moon.

'Let's run again!' I cry, starting to run as I glance

back behind me to see if the moon has heard and is intending to follow. We rush past Aunt Luscha's house, then the Big House, where Uncle Frans lives, turn off by the milk-shed, dive down under the bridge up to the barn, tear past the gloomy crossbar of the cattle-well, past the spiky, helmeted bell-tower on the stables – on and on and on. We fly so swiftly, we become invisible, like a breeze sweeping along the road, the twilight swallowing the tramp of my boots, which can't really keep up.

Darkness falls rapidly. Suddenly I find the moon on my left above tree-tops, which flicker like fencing as he runs along them. Then he's already ahead of us. In the end I stop, sweating and out of breath. It's impossible to catch up with the moon. He has won.

I find it difficult to express in words everything I have taken in with my eyes, ears, nose and mouth: the swift race, the evening twilight, the moon racing us, the gurgling of the melting snow, the strange dance of the shadows, the mild spring air, the smell of wet clothes. I should like to express the wonder all these fill me with. I should like to do something special, stretch my hand out to the moon, take him down out of the spruce branches and really feel and taste him. My feeling of amazement and inspiration could best be expressed in an exclamation, blurted out with emphasis and directed at the whole world. Something like Oh, Oh! Yes!

But I am already sufficiently a person to the extent that I make an effort to find a more involved way of expressing myself.

'We ran! Phew! The moon ran – terrifically!' I manage to blurt out, panting.

We have come to the small slope in front of our house, where the ice-cellar is. The elephant is there, a short distance away from the road in a pool of melted snow, the water up to his knees. He is standing quite still, outlined like a little smoky grey shadow against the pale snowdrifts. He has stood there for a long time –

always – just as the moon has, just as spring, Bernt and I myself have always existed. His mysterious doings fill me with acute curiosity.

'The elephant!' I say, pointing at the pool.

'Let's go and look,' says Bernt, and we wade out into the snow towards the trees by the ice-cellar, where the elephant stands watching us in silence. There's water underneath the snow and our footprints quickly darken and fill with icy, lead-grey slush.

'Come on, Riki!' says Bernt, and we climb up on to a bare stone ledge, slippery and dangerous. The whole forest is full of water gushing out of the ground and rising up through the snow, the spruces standing with their feet in water.

'We've come to see you,' I say to the elephant.

He stands quite still and silent, listening, far too busy to allow himself to be disturbed, the moonlight glistening in his dark eye like a drop of honey. He holds his head down and his trunk lowered into the water between his forelegs, a moon glistening between them at the bottom of the pool.

We hold our breath and listen with the elephant. The water gurgles again, gushing out of the ground everywhere in the darkness around us, sucking itself up through the snow, rising out of all the cracks and holes in the earth and filling all the hollows and ditches, spreading out and running all over the meadows and woods. It's a flood like the Deluge.

I realize the elephant is profoundly worried. The water is already up to his knees and still rising. He hasn't time to talk to us. He has to watch the melting snow and listen to the water rising. He stands so quietly unmoving. Is he making magic?

'If the water rises too much we'll get a boat so you can get in it and row,' I say, patting him on his purple-edged saddle-cloth. Oh, how I do like him – though he's not mine but Bernt's – his grey, plush-soft skin rug, his firm, sturdy body, his wise peppercorn eyes. We have slept in the same bed, pressed close to each other, and I have ridden on his humpy back. Once upon a time he came to see me, vast and overwhelming like a god, and he spoke to me in a human voice. But I remember that only dimly – because he has really always stood without moving since the beginning of time.

The elephant doesn't reply but goes on watching the glint of the moon-coin in the water. Then it gets darker and darker, the moon losing his golden glow and taking on a white, silvery colour. His light gets brighter and brighter, as if delicate veils of cobwebs were filling the air all round us. The melting snow gurgles.

2

EVEN THE SMALLEST THING HAS A FACE. I DON'T HAVE TO look at anything for long before its face appears, lines and surfaces joining up and adjusting so that a pair of eyes and a mouth are formed.

All the houses round my home have faces. Aunt Luscha's house is brown and dirty grey and has a crooked care-worn expression. The Big House is grave and broad-shouldered like a patriarch. The Falkenheimer aunts' house has a warm, inviting expression, but at the same time smiles craftily and slyly like a fox, and Uncle Alfred's house, which hides under an archway of dark spruces, wears a straw hat and dark glasses.

Yet they resemble neither human nor animal faces. They are simply houses and have house-faces. They may well have many pairs of eyes and many mouths, their noses may look out on one side, and inside the big face you suddenly find small faces staring at you in their own strange way.

There is a screen which is always put in front of our beds when we are ill. That screen seems to have stood beside me at a time of which I have no memory at all. When I woke up and started seeing, my soul painted the first delicate pictures on the coarse, golden brown material of the screen, and the patterns on it are still the basic pattern for my dreams. When I close my eyes, it appears out of the darkness that fills my inner being and I see the dream pictures slowly appearing. What have I not seen in the strange, colourful pattern of the screen? It's like looking in a book that never comes to an end, and where the whole world is portrayed in a veiled and mysterious way.

I see church spires, stairs, portals, wriggling dragons, red-eyed elephants, pale moons, boats, fruits and teasels. There are pretty little birds there, too, with purple beaks, which are at the same time crosses on graves, and laciniated branches which are also women and spiky monsters. The colourful polygons merge together, divide themselves up and turn themselves into almost anything. They move as if they were alive, the one figure reaching out after the other. The one pursues, the others flee, a third sits still and waits. There's a meaning and a connection between them as in a story, a rhythmical movement as in a dance. In between, you come to a point where everything begins again in an eternal circle.

I can lie for hours looking at the screen and giving different interpretations to whatever I see.

3

IT IS ANIMALS I LOVE, ANIMALS THAT LOVE ME. ANIMALS talk to me and keep me company. They think the same thoughts as I do and delight in and regret the same things. Their presence gives me a sense of well-being and safety experienced only in the company of kindred creatures. Animals once carried me out of the night of no memories and stood in a circle round my cradle when my eyes slowly opened and found the strength to see. They brought me up and cared for me, played with me and lulled me to sleep. People are something alien and distant, and shadow-like, only touching the very edges of my existence.

The rain is what I remember most clearly from my life among the animals.

It always seemed to be raining – terrible rain with endless streams of water, rustling as if through the strainer of a huge watering-can. All this water falling through the pale-grey air makes your eyes darken. The animals go around deeply troubled by the wet, their faces glistening with moisture, and some are dressed in rubber raincoats, others wearing galoshes. The rhinoceros has put up an umbrella and is standing at a crossroads talking about the weather to a hippopotamus he has met quite by chance.

Then we walk round in the rain, wondering, listening to the song of the drainpipes and the dark thumps of the drips. We see the long, sharp shafts falling through the air and making holes in the puddles. They splash up from the edge of the pavement like fine powder and make the windows opaque, as if covered with fish scales. The ground turns wet and glistening and our bodies are reflected as if we were walking on dark, polished wood.

The rain is terrible. Our whole house might be flooded and float away like a ship. We walk a long way away. The rhinoceros jabs the umbrella into the ground and it is turned into a gigantic mushroom. We seek shelter under it while the rivulets murmur around us and the rain rustles among the ferns. When it grows lighter, the rhinoceros pulls up the mushroom and it becomes an umbrella again. We continue our walk. Everywhere we go, horse-tail plants shoot up out of the ground, covering it like a forest of pale-green rain-trees, and we feed on their sweet cones during the journey.

Another time, we are crossing the town in a cab. The cab is so full of all kinds of animals, we can hardly squeeze in. The animals sit curled up on top of each other, the smaller ones on top of the bigger ones, and all the time we are afraid one of them will fall out. The plush-grey elephant with his purple-edged saddle-cloth is there too. He is so large, he can scarcely fit into the cab and we are frightened the bench under him will break. We are in a terrible hurry – I've forgotten what we were going to do – but we're very happy. It's like a carnival.

Then there's Christmas. The light floods over us and dazzles our eyes. We can't take in all that magnificence and all the glitter that fills the room. We enter the palace of the King of the Elephants. Grandmother sits down to play the piano and the people and animals around me all sing. Then the elephant hands me one pink and one pale-green slice of crystallized fruit, both as transparent as glass, the surface glittering like a star from the countless grains of sugar. The elephant is so terribly big, his head is at the same level as the top of the Christmas tree and this time he is as gruesome as an idol.

Suddenly I am alone. The animals have slipped out of our house without my really knowing how they did it. They stay there in their distant, godlike world where only my thoughts can push their way in, and they take no notice of my calling them and asking them to come back. The memory of our friendship fills me with a light feeling of happiness mixed with a melancholy sense of loss. I live in the hope that they will show themselves again, and expect to see them suddenly reappear during my wanderings through the shadowy great rooms, then our reunion will be fulfilled. The thought of them often gives me no rest, filling me with a constant longing, but also with the happy knowledge of a more godlike and free existence than has been mine. A human being who had once lived and been friends with the gods but had then been abandoned, must have felt like that.

4

I DON'T REALLY KNOW WHAT KIND OF PERSON I AM. I JUST know that there is something called 'I' when it talks to itself, though it is neither seen nor heard – and that there are all kinds of other things seen and heard and yet not entirely real because they can't speak to themselves in that silent way. But I can take on all kinds of guises and am by no means forced to appear in human form. I can turn myself at will into different kinds of animals or horrible creatures. I can float above the world, invisible to everyone, and look down on the forests, fields, cattle and people below. I enclose the ground, the air and the sky inside me and fill the space so there is nothing outside me. I am present everywhere, infinite and omnipotent. It is I who have created the world.

I live for long periods turned into a gigantic snake. To start with, I extend my full length all the way to

Viborg, which is infinitely far away at the end of the Viborg road – the longest of all roads leading away from my home. Then they tell me Helsinki is even further away, so I hurriedly turn myself into an even bigger snake. Nothing may be bigger than I am. It doesn't matter I am so big that the whole world would fit into me, or that I can neither see nor count all the coils along my body when I glance back. I can easily go round our house and take up no more room than the others who live there. I reign absolutely over my home and over the world and everyone has to obey me. When I curl up, Grandmother and Mamma can take me in their arms and feed me with milk and biscuits. But I am very easily vexed. I gobble up Grandmother, Mamma and Pappa and all the other occupants of the house several times a day. I rush at them with my mouth wide open, as wide as the sky, and let them feel the terror of annihilation.

Pappa once came into the nursery and asked Bernt and me to come into the dining-room where the grown-ups were having dinner. He said a new aunt had come to our home, a nurse all of our own who had come to look after us. I stepped up to the table after Bernt. There she was, in a white blouse, her dark hair in a knot at the back of her neck, and she had a completely strange face you knew nothing about and which might be unpleasant or dangerous. But actually I really rather liked it, for it was young and smooth and there were no wrinkles to be afraid of.

'Say good-evening and say who you are,' said Pappa.

'I'm the Giant Snake, from here to Helsinki,' I said, taking a step back.

She smiled and held out her hand to touch me, but I quickly wriggled out of reach. When the others began to laugh, I crawled hissing under the table. But the new aunt didn't leave me in peace. She lifted up the fringes of the table-cloth, looked down under the table and laughed. Then she fumbled with her hand to pull me to her. She clearly had no idea how to be afraid. I was furious, shot along the whole of my terrible length and blew at her a red flame that rapidly consumed her.

5

I REMEMBER AND SEE GROWN-UPS ONLY IN FRAGMENTS, LIKE pieces of a jigsaw puzzle. Some of the pieces are missing, so I can't fit them all together. I see faces with changing expressions, hands touching me, laps I climb up on to, stomachs and waistcoat buttons, gold chains and necklaces I fiddle with. I see hems of skirts sweeping past and boots tramping heavily across the floorboards, but I find it difficult deciding to whom they belong and putting the parts together into a whole. They are as tall as trees and wherever they go they make the floor tremble with the weight of their steps. When they get up from a chair, their heads brush the ceiling, and when they go through a doorway I am frightened they will hit their heads on the top of the frame.

I have a complete picture only of Bernt, no one else. He is in proportion and neat, although considerably bigger than I am. Like me, he is wearing a dark jersey with a red band right across his chest, and a pair of short trousers enclose his round backside. When we go out, we each have a pointed pixie cap on our heads. His is blue and mine is red.

The whole of this complicated world of people, animals and everything else is there for our sake. Although I am undeniably the one who is the central point of existence and who gives meaning to everything,

Bernt comes next to me in importance and significance. He is my brother in the same way as the moon is the brother of the sun and comes next in rank after the sun.

6

OF ALL THESE PEOPLE, MAMMA GIVES ME THE GREATEST sense of physical closeness.

I sometimes sleep in her room, a long, rather dark room, with one window that is shaded by the dark spruce branches outside. The room is full of a running darkness, like a shower of ashes. A dark rug, as heavy and coarse as the darkness itself, is stretched across the window to keep out the light, which trickles in small, trembling grains through the sacking-like material.

Before I fall asleep, the darkness rings in my ears, stronger and stronger, so that I become quite deaf. The walls wobble, the floor under my bed disappears and with the black flakes of darkness I hurtle down into the depths called sleep which have no memory.

Sometimes I lie in Mamma's bed. I see her breasts in front of me – they hang like heavy fruits out of the circle of lace of her unbuttoned nightgown. They are criss-crossed with blue veins and at the end of them are nipples like two wrinkled, brown cones. I know that at one time long ago I used to take them in my mouth and suck them, but nowadays the thought fills me with a sense of discomfort and deep shame. I am afraid they will touch me. I'm no longer a baby like Tommy. Until quite recently, he used to lie there sucking them, and I think they're still glistening from his spit. That makes them even more unpleasant. Cow's milk tastes much better, and also your bigs are pale yellow like an infant's when you drink Mamma's milk. I've seen Tommy's myself out there on the rubbish-heap when they empty the chamber-pot, like the little balls of dough and the pretzels Kirsti makes on the kitchen table when she is baking, and I remember that long ago I too used to do bigs like that. But nowadays I do black ones like grown-ups. That's much grander and they're all afraid of them.

Mamma's body is soft and warm, her skin so silky it's a lovely feeling lying under the covers, pressing up against it. But an extraordinary sharp smell comes from her, and it stubbornly sticks to her nightgown and bedclothes. It reminds me of the smell of prunes and something else very familiar which I can't place. Something animal in that smell frightens me – like those nipples.

There's a picture on the wall above Mamma's bed of a young woman with a naked, fair, curly-haired boy in her arms, a mother and her son. The mother is only half visible; she has lovely reddish-blonde hair over her shoulders, her face narrow and gentle, the lines of her throat and chin reminiscent of a roe-deer. She is wearing a light-coloured costume with wide sleeves, thin and transparent, and in the neckline you can see the shadows between her breasts. Her slim hands are held carefully round the boy's chubby, naked body. He is standing in her arms with his little backside half turned towards you as you look and his fingers are on her neckline. Apples, pears and apricots hang all round them, glowing like little baby bottoms out of the green foliage. I don't know why I like that picture so much, but I often creep up and stand on the bed looking at it, although I know that's forbidden in daytime when the white bedspread is on.

Actually, I really like the young woman in the picture more than my own mother. Sometimes I take off all my clothes, throw them down on the bed and then step naked into the picture. I put myself into the young woman's arms and take the boy's place. I can feel her hands stroking my body, caressing and tender, and she breathes on me, pressing me to her breast and finally smothering me with kisses.

But the picture isn't mine. It is Pappa's. He bought it and hung it up above Mamma's bed. He really likes it and says the young mother in the picture looks like an angel. Sometimes he takes me in his arms and lets me look at it. 'The eternal woman!' he says. 'Remember, a mother's love is the greatest and most sacred in the world.'

7

PAPPA IS QUITE UNLIKE ALL THE OTHERS. FOR LONG spells he can be as invisible as the moon, so you almost forget he exists, but then suddenly he is there again and the whole house is quite changed. No longer is anything as before. So there is always something exciting and secretive about him – you never know what will happen and what surprises he has in store.

Suddenly he unwraps brown paper from a parcel and takes out a decapitated billy-goat's head with crafty, peering eyes. He hangs it up in the living-room above the piano. Or else out of his coat pocket he takes a gigantic oval mirror in which Mamma's and Grandmother's heads bounce up and down in alarm and the whole room, its table, teacups, cupboards and music-stand, are about to tip over in it. Like a conjuror, he takes little trees, flowers and bunches of grapes out of his pockets. A head-dress of colourful feathers for Bernt and a knight's black shield with golden stars on it for me.

In the morning, when you come running into the dining-room, you don't recognize it. The piano is along another wall, tables and chairs have been moved around and there are new and unfamiliar pictures on the walls.

Pappa lifts up cupboards and sofas as if they were toys, waking pieces of furniture out of their torpor and making them walk around the house. When they get up, they become dark and tall like monsters, swaying menacingly as they stride on. They get stuck in doorways, whimper, shriek and stamp when they can't squeeze through. I get frightened and rush into the nursery to hide.

Pappa wears glasses. They are much bigger than ordinary eyes and their look is much sharper and more penetrating. Sometimes he looks like the dog in the fairy story with eyes as big as saucers. When he takes his glasses off, he can't see anything. He fumbles with his hand on the table and sticks his nose in the open book as if sniffing at it. His face becomes unfamiliar and naked, a fiery red line appearing between his eyebrows, his cheeks longer and his eyes small and peering. Pappa has a moustache under his nose and it tickles when he kisses you. He smells of tobacco and honey. He eats and drinks smoke, and now and again spews out bluish puffs like a chimney, so you gasp and cough if you stand too close to him.

Sometimes Pappa takes us to the bath-house when he goes swimming. First he takes his clothes off and dances and leaps round the heap of clothing like a savage. He lifts his arms and slaps them round his shoulders as if he were hugging himself. Then he comes roaring like a railway engine along the jetty and suddenly he has gone. When I turn round, I see him floating high up above the lake. He rises in a great arch, higher and higher, as if about to fly straight into the sun, and not until he is far, far away, almost on the opposite shore where the belt of reeds starts, does he fall and plunge into the waves. A shimmering rainbow flares up above the water where he has vanished.

He sits on the diving-board with his head between his knees like a Red Indian. 'A man once,' he says, 'a man once sat on a jetty – and fell asleep. And suddenly. . .!'

He falls backwards, spins round like a pretzel and disappears beneath a column of foam. A whole eternity goes by while I stare down at the circles in the water getting wider and wider and white bubbles gurgling up from the place where Pappa has disappeared. I wonder if he will ever come back, or has he hidden himself for ever down in the black depths under the jetty? Then suddenly – just when I have already abandoned all hope – to my amazement and delight, his face shoots up out of the water, spluttering and blinking.

Occasionally Pappa comes into the nursery in the evening when we are already in bed and have been told to be quiet and try to go to sleep. 'Good-evening, Kangaroo!' he says, laughing and running his hand over my head.

At once, I'm no longer a child but a little kangaroo boy with reddish-brown fur and long, upright ears. When Pappa puts me down on the edge of my bed to go over to Bernt and repeat the trick, I dare not move, so strange and alien does my whole body feel. Instead of hands, I have sweet little paws that I swing down and hold up in front of my chest, my long, folded hind legs have black claws and, instead of a face, I have a long, hairy nose like a calf's.

'Now we'll dance the Kangaroo Dance!' says Pappa.

We start dancing the Kangaroo Dance, Bernt and I. It goes in dizzy leaps, round and round the room, from the edge of the bed right across the table and armchairs, down on to the sofa, up again over the wash-stand and the bedhead, down among the cushions on Aunt's bed, past the lamp-holder up on the wardrobe and down again – to and fro, back and forth, hither and thither. Like balls, we bounce round the room, our stomachs fizzing with delight and terror, and we scream with laughter. Sometimes I close my eyes, frightened of hitting the ceiling or the lamp. Pappa constantly transforms himself, changing character, one moment a kangaroo pappa gathering us up in his arms, the next a tree in whose branches we dance, the next moment flinging us out into space like a Titan, then becoming a mountain peak on which we land during our breath-taking journey through the air. It is much more fun and more exciting being a kangaroo than a boy, and I wish this kangaroo life of ours would never come to an end.

But the same creature who is the source of so much joy can also be terrible and as horrible as a wolf.

I go with Pappa to the forest to cut stakes for a fence and on the way home I am allowed to carry the axe. When I get behind and it starts growing dark, I amuse myself by striking the axe against a stone to watch the sparks flying in the darkness.

The following morning a creature comes towards me from the other end of the living-room, tall and black as a post. Its face is awful, its eyes glowing with rage and hatred, and it fills the whole room with its furious shouts. I don't remember what happened next. But after I had gone out and had stopped crying, I tell Bernt that Pappa had wanted to chop my head off with the axe I had ruined.

8

BERNT KNOWS EVERYTHING ABOUT TROPICAL PRIMEVAL forests, cyclones and volcanoes. He can tell you about icebergs and penguins, about the moon that pulls the water in the ocean behind it so that there is ebb and flow. Together with Mamma, he has lived inside the mountain with the dwarfs, he has seen a cep mushroom as big as a tree and underneath it a white forest deer with round eyes and a mouth like a crescent. He has sailed across the octopus waters to America and has learnt from the Red Indians how to track animals. He goes about with a notebook in his pocket and draws the funny patterns left behind by the paws and claws of animals in the snow-drifts round the house. And he can see whether it has been a rat, or a crow or even a wolf, where it has come from and where it has since gone. He once met Death himself skiing out on the ice in a black cloak and silver-braided livery.

I like Bernt because he knows so much and I would rather be with him than alone. I usually go with him when he climbs over the fence to the meadow and sets off on a journey of exploration. Sometimes we have to crawl down into a ditch and hold our breath so as to see the swarms of birds better as they circle above the meadow and land in a furrow a little way away from us. Bernt knows what their flight means, why they flap and twitter like that, and he writes down everything in his notebook. I like him because he helps me when my galosh gets stuck in the mud, when a branch pulls my cap off, or when I fall over and muddy my coat. I like him because he can read. When we look in the animal book, he can tell me that the big, bright-red parrot with the white cheeks is called a Macaw, and the funny brown-and-white speckled bird with the huge tuft of feathers on its head, which is like Struwwelpeter, is called the Hoopoe, and the queenly one with a crow's head and a beautiful pale-blue ballgown with a silvery train is called Archduke Rudolf's Bird of Paradise.

But I don't like Bernt because he tells me what he did and what it was like when I didn't exist. Because I have always existed and the World can't exist without me, so he is lying when he says that. I don't like Mamma calling to him so often and letting him sit on the sofa beside her while I am put to bed. Nor do I like it that he is so often ill and then Mamma moves him into her bedroom and strokes his head. I get angry when he is given ham sandwiches, biscuits and stewed plums, for when I want some, they say I mustn't be mean and all that is good for Bernt, because he has such a weak stomach.

Most of all, I don't like him because he is bigger and stronger than I am, and is always saying I must obey him. Whenever none of the grown-ups can see us and I find something that's fun to do, like stamping and splashing in a puddle, filling my mouth with stones, or chasing the chickens and frightening them, Bernt always comes and tells me not to do it. He makes me do all kinds of things I think are boring, like carrying stones and spruce branches for his wigwam, or lying absolutely still in the moss and being a marmot when he goes hunting. I don't in the least like letting him shoot at me with his catapult, being dead, and letting him cut great pieces out of my body and eating me up, without my being allowed to make the slightest sound.

If I don't do what he tells me, he pushes me over or lies on top of me and hits and pulls me about. If I fight back and bite his thumb or pull a tuft of hair out of his head, the grown-ups scold me and tell me not to fight. Sometimes when he hits me and it really hurts, I get so angry I don't know what I'm doing. I fly at him and cling on hard with my hands and teeth, biting and scratching, and I don't let go although blows are hailing down on me.

Once when Bernt turned his back on me, I picked up a big stone – it was so big I would otherwise have hardly been able to tip it over on to its side, but anger had given me the strength of a giant. I flung it as hard as I could at Bernt's head. Although the stone hit him and bounced back with a thump, his head wasn't crushed and Bernt didn't sink dead to the ground in an immobile heap at my feet as I had hoped. But there was quite a lot of blood running down his face, spotting his blouse and making his hair stick together in streaky wisps. Bernt had to go to Grandmother's room, where Mamma and Grandmother washed and plastered him up and wound a white bandage round his head. Grandmother said I was Cain the brother murderer and showed me the picture of the handsome young Abel lying stretched out on the ground with his eyes closed and his forehead spotted with blood. Then she stood me in the corner.

Another time we were both sitting on our pots in the nursery after dinner. I don't like that, because Mamma doesn't let you get up until you have done something in the pot and that's often very difficult. Sometimes nothing comes at all, however much you push and press, and sometimes just a little bobble like a hare's dropping is swimming around when you get up to show what you have done. Mamma says that's not enough and orders you to sit down again. If I then start scooting round the room to pass the time, looking at the knot-hole eyes in the timbered walls or examining the turned legs of the desk, Bernt yells at me to sit still and that it's forbidden to scoot around like that. But this time everything went very quickly. I felt at once something very big coming out of me and falling into the pot. When I started to get up, Bernt shouted that I mustn't.

'But I've finished,' I said.

'No,' said Bernt, who was still squatting down. 'You haven't done anything.'

'Yes I have. I can get up.'

'No, your potty's quite empty,' said Bernt. 'And if you try to get up again, I'll call Mamma.'

I was so enraged, I simply saw red. I got up, grabbed the pot and flung it at Bernt as hard as I could.

I was birched on my bare bottom for that. They took me just as I was with my trousers unbuttoned and down. A huge, fat bundle of birch twigs appeared from nowhere, the leaves and catkins still on them, and Grandmother put me across her knee. I screamed and kicked and cried but didn't succeed in getting free. It stung as if Grandmother had beaten me with a bunch of nettles. Though the pain wasn't the worst. What was worse was that Grandmother suddenly looked like a wicked witch. There are witches who turn children into pigs by beating them with a birch and then shutting them in a cage to fatten them so their flesh gets really tender and juicy. And Grandmother repeated over and over again between blows: 'You're a little pig! A really horrible little pig, that's what you are.'

9

TOMMY IS SO SMALL YOU FEEL ASHAMED TO LOOK AT HIM. His clothes are never right on him, the buttons never done up, his shoes always lost, his socks falling half-way down his calves and always waving about loose at the toes like a pixie hat. His nose is always running and he also often wets his trousers.

Tommy walks unsteadily as if he were on the deck of a rolling ship. Every now and again he stops, waves his arms about and sits down with thump on his backside. When he tries to run after me, he falls headlong and lets out his usual furious howl. He doesn't try to get up, but just lies there, opening his mouth wide in terror and howling so that it makes your head ache. Although I have done nothing wrong, some grown-up, Mamma or Aunt, comes rushing up, looks angrily at me and asks why Tommy is yelling like that. Tommy is afraid and starts screaming for the slightest thing: when Uncle

Georg comes into the hall, when a cup or plate falls to the floor and breaks, or when he catches sight of a worm or a daddy-long-legs. It's absolutely impossible to play with him without sooner or later doing something that will set him off howling. He screams as soon as you take anything he has in his hand or he's sucking, even if it's your very own toy.

I remember a time when Tommy could walk only if he was holding on to a chair and pushing it in front of him. He mostly crawled about on all fours like a puppy. He eats sand and mud, tears up any books and newspapers he manages to pull off the shelves, and he chews the dolls' heads so their tops buckle in and their faces get full of cracks and holes. He puts buttons and nails into his mouth, tries to put bits of cloth and ends of wool into his nose or peas into his ears, and the grown-ups are always busy watching over him and pulling all kinds of extraordinary objects out of his insides.

I think it's shameful to behave like that, even if you are little and have no sense. I can't understand why the grown-ups go to so much trouble over him and don't give him away instead, as he is nothing but a nuisance. But the grown-ups think the opposite and delight in him and always smile in such a friendly way when he totters into the room. When you're with him, they all just look at him and talk about him. He goes from one to the next to be hugged. All of them hold out their arms to him. All of them want to hold him, kiss and cuddle him.

That's because he's a Sunday's child and was born with a shirt on like an angel. Bernt and I came into the world without a stitch on to cover us and, what's more, on a perfectly ordinary weekday. Sunday's children are full of grace and everyone loves them. Everything on earth is kind to them and protects them, all creatures are pleased and happy when they see them and talk to them. They are friends of the flowers, the birds and the stars. When they grow up, they become princes, are given a scarlet velvet suit, a golden crown on their heads, and the most beautiful royal daughter as consort.

I don't like it at all and so keep away as much as I can from Tommy. I think he's silly, a nuisance and unpleasant. I would never ever want to be him or behave like him – you feel ashamed when you think that you had once been just as small and perhaps like him. He's nothing special and he doesn't really interest me much. We also don't have much to do with each other, because he spends most of his time with Njanjan in his nursery, or with Mamma in the bedroom. He's too small to come with Bernt and me when we go out to play. He stays lying on the floor sucking different coloured bricks, which he then throws away one by one, as if not a single one tasted good enough.

I also think it's peculiar that Tommy is always so scared and that he screams such a lot, although he's a Sunday's child. If all creatures and things love him and wish him well, why is he frightened by next to nothing? He's always hanging on to Mamma, tottering after her everywhere, clutching with both hands to her skirts as if the most important thing in the world was never to let go. Sometimes when Mamma walks quickly, he stumbles, falls over and is dragged along for a while. As soon as Mamma manages to get free and close the door behind her, his face takes on an expression of the most profound terror and he starts up his usual wail. And it doesn't make any difference when Njanjan comes rushing in, gathers him up in her arms and carries him away. The howls go on behind the closed door, as if they would never end.

Sometimes Mamma takes Tommy with her when we go to the bath-house. Tommy keeps squatting down to pick something up off the road. When Mamma lets go of his hand and walks on ahead a few steps, he throws everything down and rushes wailing after us with his arms outstretched, his face all creased like an old dwarf's. Then he loses a shoe and falls over in the dust on the road.

It's just the same at the bath-house. As soon as Mamma has undressed Tommy, he starts screaming, rushes away from the water and tries to hide in a corner. Finally, Mamma takes him in her arms and goes down the steps that disappear into the dark, lapping water. Tommy struggles, grabbing wildly at the neck of Mamma's bathing-costume, her shoulders, her hair. But that makes no difference – three times Mamma dips him into the lead-grey waves. His little body disappears into a silvery, shimmering swirl of foam and you can see nothing but his terrified wide-open eyes, rigid like a fish's, and his gaping mouth that can't get a sound out but is just gasping for air.

I look on with a kind of grim curiosity and a feeling of secret satisfaction. It's good that Tommy is so contemptible and afraid of water, that Mamma is stronger than he is and his struggles and shrieks don't help in the slightest.

It's good that Mamma does that, because he's a Sunday's child.

10

OUR NURSE IS REALLY CALLED AUNT ADÈLE, BUT WE JUST call her Aunt, because she is our very own aunt and is only there for the sake of Bernt and me. She washes us and dresses us, fetches our food and makes sure we get to the chamber-pot in time to pee. She reads stories to us and shows us picture books, comes with us when we go for a walk and sleeps with us in the nursery. She is the one who decides when we may get up and when we have to go to bed, when we must come and eat, when we may play and when we have to go for a walk along the road. It is she who says what you can do and it is from her we have to ask permission before we can do anything, to make sure we don't expose ourselves to the most horrible accidents.

She's the same aunt who was consumed by my flaming breath. But the roles have now been reversed and I'm almost the one who have to be afraid of her. From having been a strange aunt coming from God knows where and hardly even really existing, today she has grown and become more and more omnipotent, so now life would be inconceivable without her. But deep down I still know, despite everything, that her power is limited, and it is I myself who have conferred that power on her, so in exchange she will look after me and would stop existing the very same day I didn't need her.

Aunt is tall and slim like a tree. Her head with its hard knot of hair at the back is so high up that it seems quite small when you look from below. In the winter she wears a long coat with a fur collar, a square fur cap and she holds a muff in front of her. Everything she has on is black. When it snows, the snowflakes stick to the fur and she becomes speckled like a silver fox.

In the summer Aunt wears a black skirt and a white blouse with half-length sleeves and round, black buttons that look like berries. When she goes into town, she gets out a pair of white gloves and a gigantic black hat with a horribly long hatpin. The gloves are fine and narrow like tobacco flowers. Aunt pulls them on to her hands and up her forearms. She tries on the hat, which reminds me of an umbrella, in front of the mirror, and then sticks that awful hatpin right through her head so that its point sticks out like a nail at her temple.

After breakfast, we put on our outdoor clothes and set off for the forest, which looks so dark and dangerous when you see it from the nursery window. But you needn't be at all afraid to walk in it when Aunt is with you. There are so many amazing things in the forest:

wood shavings and spruce-needles, fern leaves and slimy brown slugs. It's as murky and damp as a cellar, the tree-trunks so tall they go right up to the clouds and their dark branches are as high as a church roof.

At last we come to the foot of the mountain. There are terrible precipices there, a blood-red cliff-face, and huge, silent boulders squat on the ledges looking sternly at you. The ground is silvery grey and covered with lichens. Black holes leading down into the underworld gape at you everywhere, and down there live dangerous, unknown creatures. Aunt helps me when the moss gives way and I start sliding down the steep cliff-face, or when my sandal gets caught between two crafty loose boulders. She holds out her hand and pulls me up on to the ledge on which she is standing. Then she brushes the needles and moss off my knees, where my stockings have acquired two dirty wet patches.

When we have climbed up the mountain, Aunt sits down on a boulder and takes out a book or her knitting. Bernt builds his wigwam and I get down into a crevice among the bog bilberry, Labrador tea and cotton-grass to wait for the little green butterfly that will come to see me. When he comes flying along, you don't see that he is green at all. He is greyish brown like a piece of bark and its hard even to see him as he flutters along the ground. Sometimes you think you've just got a shadow in your eye, but when he lands on a Labrador tea flower and closes his wings, he's a lovely pale-green colour like a leaf. I sit absolutely still so as not to frighten him and look at him combing his antennae, waving his forepaws about and signalling to me that he likes me. He has a long tongue, as fine as cotton thread. He dips it into the hairy flowers, rolls it up like a clock spring, then flutters away and has gone, but he's only joking, for suddenly he's back again, sitting looking at me, swaying slowly on a grass stem. He once settled on my hand and sat there for a few moments, quite still, tickling the back of my hand, but I didn't dare move or breathe in case he flew away.

It is so lovely up there on the mountain and I am happy and pleased the sun is shining, the sky so high and big, the little butterfly my friend, and Aunt is sitting quite close to me on her boulder so I can see her all the time.

Sometimes we walk across velvety green tussocks of moss covered with chickweed wintergreen, long-leaved stitchwort and may lily, over to the waterfall. The nearer we get, the louder its voice becomes. It roars and sighs, hisses and sizzles invisibly ahead of us. The trees are taller and closer together, the air darker. The ground is completely covered with needles, an agaric mushroom glistening here and there behind a rotting stump. When we come out on to the cliff edge where the water is rushing in foaming white grooves, parting, wriggling between the boulders and reuniting again, the roar is so loud I can't hear what Aunt and Bernt are saying. You just see them moving their lips and pointing hither and thither. It's cold and damp. The watercourse is edged with tall grasses, ferns and marsh plants. Rays of the sun break here and there through the spruce branches, making the cobwebs between stems of plants and drops of water floating in the air glitter and shimmer.

The longer I stand looking and listening to the roar, the more peculiar I feel. The waterfall doesn't speak with one voice but with a thousand large voices and small voices – some thunder and growl, others ripple and gurgle, splashing and swishing, murmuring like guttering, hissing like a kettle and roaring like the wind in a storm. Sometimes it sounds like Grandmother or Pappa playing the piano at home. It's also funny to look at all the spouting mouths through which the waterfall is speaking. Some spew out cascades of smouldering white foam, others a reflecting arch of water that is quite transparent, others shoot out silvery, shimmering spurts of water like icicles, and out of others well a shower of rustling dark drops. It's fun to look down into the streams of water incessantly rushing past, to follow the twists and turns and divisions of the current, and to see the way the water digs itself down beneath the roots of the trees and ripples up out of secretive black holes in the earth. The bulging shapes below the waterfall are filled with absolutely black water where sticks, bubbles and flakes of foam dance around in an eternal circle. It's fun to scoop up the white foam like whipped cream floating on the water, to hold it in your hand and feel how light it is, to taste it, then blow on it, making it burst and sail away in the form of big white flakes. I never want to leave this secret place, and Aunt has to shake me until I realize we have to go home.

I like Aunt because she is young and good-looking. No one chats and laughs so much as she does. No one takes me into her arms so often, no one else tells me so many stories or shows me so many pictures. She tells me about how the girl Baby squeezed her eyes shut and thought no one could see her when she had to sit on her pot in a railway compartment. She tells me about her brother, who used to cut into dead people to see what was inside them. She also tells me about the ungodly lady who hung up a hammock between two chimneys and swung high up under the clouds, smoking cigarettes, laughing and shouting mocking words at God. But when the rope broke, she hurtled down from the roof and broke her back and was paralysed for the rest of her life.

When I need help, I can always turn to Aunt. She helps me tell my left foot from my right, tie my shoelaces, find my lost toys. She protects me from Bernt when he is nasty and wants to hit me. But most of all I like her because she has said she likes me best.

Aunt is rather impatient. If you're disobedient, or you don't do what she says immediately, she may pull your hair so hard it hurts long afterwards. Or else she shakes you, or tweaks your ear – and a few times she has even smacked my bottom. But that's not too bad and I soon forget it because she's usually so nice afterwards. It's much worse when she stands me in the corner, or sends me to bed, or leaves me with no pudding, and is so cross she doesn't even look at me or speak to me. Because then it's as if I didn't exist at all.

Although it's obvious she likes me best, and actually everyone ought to do that, all the same I'm rather pleased and proud that she does. But it's troublesome and difficult always being just as she wants you to be so that she can like you. I have to pay attention all the time to make sure she doesn't stop liking me.

She insists that I must never cry. 'A big man like you', she snorts, 'screaming and crying like a woman! What'll become of you?'

I am fearfully ashamed and feel like sinking into the ground, and yet I can't help crying. Of course I'm glad Aunt thinks I'm so big and clever. But it's awfully difficult and dull being a man all the time, never crying when someone hurts you, never being afraid or frightened, doing your buttons up yourself and never messing yourself. Sometimes when I get really cross, I don't bother at all to try to be a man and I don't care if Aunt sighs and shakes her head and says: 'I don't think we'll ever make a man of you!' It feels really good to be able to do just what I feel like, crying, yelling and kicking and being really naughty. But afterwards it always feels as if some awful accident had happened and I would never ever be happy again. I don't dare look Aunt in the eye and all the time have to think that perhaps she won't bother about me any longer. I'm afraid she will tell all the others about me so that they will all stop liking me.

Worst of all is when I do bigs in my trousers – though that doesn't happen very often these days. Once it happened on a Sunday morning when Aunt had dressed me in my Sunday best white trousers and we were out walking in the meadow to pick daisies. I wanted to call for help, but realized at once the accident had already happened. I dared not move, but just stood still looking at Aunt and Bernt bending over among the flowers, and feeling that terrible voluptuous sense of warm dampness inside my trousers.

It was dreadful then to have to limp home holding Aunt's hand, to see the anger and disgust on her face, to bend down to let her unbutton my trousers and reveal my shame in all its vileness. While Aunt carefully pulled off my trousers with the tips of her fingers and hissed at me to stand still and be quiet, I was seized with such terror that I would rather Aunt had immediately thrown me in the bucket together with the dirtied trousers. I couldn't believe she would ever overcome her loathing and bring herself to touch me, wash me and dry me. I was then put to bed. Aunt said there weren't any more trousers and I would have to run around all day with no trousers on and my shirt sticking out under my Sunday blouse. But I didn't want that, for then everyone would know what I'd done. So I crept into bed, and then realized that wouldn't make any difference, as the others would all know anyhow. Next morning, when I was given clean trousers and came out of the nursery, I didn't dare look anyone in the eye.

There's a white cross hanging above Aunt's bed, Christ's face in the middle of it. He has a crown of thorns on his head and is gazing up at the ceiling with agonized eyes. His lips are parted and dark drops of blood are trickling down his forehead. In the daytime it's a perfectly ordinary cross and in no way different from the other things in our house. But at night it glimmers like a glow-worm. When all the other things have become blurred and grey and the Christ figure in the middle of the cross has darkened to a black spot, the arms of the cross begin to radiate a soft, moonlike shimmer. The darker the room gets, the more clearly the cross is outlined above Aunt's bed – in the end the cross is the only thing left when everything else has been swallowed up by the dark. It glows and watches here in the nursery in the same way as the moon and the stars watch out there. Its light is so bright, I'm frightened.

Aunt doesn't come in until late at night. I can hear the grown-ups' conversation dying away in the living-room, the chair legs scraping against the floor and the sound of steps echoing in all directions. The narrow, golden outline of the door goes out. Aunt has a candle in her hand, the flame fluttering and leaning in the draught. At the sight of Aunt and the warm, shimmering golden halo floating above the flame, I am seized with a sense of numbing safety and well-being. I dare not say anything, but pretend to be asleep, because I know she would be upset if she noticed I was still awake.

She puts the candlestick down on the bedside table and starts undressing. She always does it in exactly the same way. First she stands at the end of the bed and pulls her dress up over her head, then she sits on the edge of the bed and takes off her shoes and stockings. She gets up again, unhooks her corset, puts it down, takes out her hairpins and shakes her head so that her hair falls down over her shoulders and frames her face like a black hood. Not until then does she take her nightgown out from under her pillow, then she raises her arms and lets it slide over her head so that the billowing white material covers her right down to her ankles. Then soon after, or almost at the same time, you can hear a few almost secretive clicks, and her daytime shift falls down and appears in the shape of a large pretzel at her feet. She steps out of it, hangs her clothes up on the chair, puts her hairpins into her mouth and starts putting up her hair for the night.

I never manage to catch sight of anything more of her body than the hollow between her breasts and the dark shadows in her armpits. I have waited many a time with excitement for a mishap to occur, her nightgown to get caught up and stop as it falls, while the day-shift has already slid down to the floor. But the trick works every single time.

Then Aunt blows out the candle. When my eyes have got used to the dark and the contours of the room begin to appear again, I can see Aunt kneeling by the bed with her back to me, her face raised towards the glowing cross. Sometimes I think she is whimpering and sniffing, but mostly she is quite silent and still. In her long nightgown she looks like a ghost. The cross above her radiates an even more horrible light. Now and again the wooden walls click, a floorboard creaks, someone patters along outside the window – but Aunt never moves. It seems as if she never intends to get up again but will stay on her knees and pray for a thousand years.

Why can't she stop? Is it all my fault? Have I been so naughty again that I've made her so unhappy not even Christ can help her? Is she praying for me to be better and kinder? Sometimes I wonder whether it is even Aunt and not a ghost kneeling there, unmoving in her white hood. I struggle with the desire to make some sound so that Aunt has to turn round, but the fear of recognizing something dreadful as the averted face turns towards me holds me back.

11

IN THE EVENING, AS THE TREES DARKEN IN THE ROSY evening glow and the eaves protrude over the windows like an increasingly darker shadow, Grandmother comes in to say evening prayers with us. She sits down in an armchair, clasps her hands and looks thoughtfully into the copper-coloured light pouring in through the window. In a subdued golden glow, the light is reflected on her forehead, her cheeks and from the clasped hands in her lap. Otherwise everything on her is black: the crocheted lace cap on her head, the wide-sleeved, high-necked costume hiding her figure in its heavy folds and covering the tips of her shoes when she is seated. Her eyes are sunk deeply into the shadow of her eye-sockets beneath the lines and tired hollows of her forehead. It is often difficult to know if they are looking at you or whether they are looking into an unknown distance no one else knows about. For Grandmother is long-sighted. She can look across at forests, mountains and lakes right to the furthest border of the world and she can see a pin that has fallen there, though she can't see it if she drops it on the floor here at home.

At first, Grandmother sings the evening hymn, her voice thin and penetrating and yet subdued like the hum of a swarm of mosquitoes at sunset. We sit up in our beds, clasp our hands and try to sing with her:

> 'Der Mond ist aufgegangen,
> Die goldnen Sternlein prangen
> Am Himmel hell und klar.
> Der Wald steht schwartz und schweiget
> Und aus den Wiesen steiget
> Der weisse Nebel wunderbar . . .'

As yet the moon has not risen, as yet no stars are visible. The rosiness of the evening is still there on the darkening edge of the forest, but the colours are already fading and soon everything will happen, thanks to the force of the song Grandmother has sung. The moon will glide soundlessly up behind the forest and the sky will be covered with golden yellow stars just like those on my own toy shield.

'Wie ist die Welt so stille
Und in der Dämmerung Hülle
So traulich und so hold . . .'

Darkness quickly falls and outside it is utterly quiet, the birds, forest and clouds all holding their breath and listening to the singing. But Grandmother clearly doesn't approve of this soundless stillness into which the world has sunk. It would seem all too desolate if it went on all night, so she goes on:

'Nur der Bach am Felsem dort
Fliesst und rauschet immer, immefort.'

And all at once the waterfall starts seething and roaring over there in the darkness of the forest, as if someone had turned on a tap. Now we know the waterfall will have no rest or peace of mind all night. If I wake up, I'll hear its familiar lulling roar just as on every other night.

After Grandmother has plunged the world into sleep in this way, and conjured up the night, she exhorts us to say our evening prayers.

We say them by ourselves and Grandmother sits listening, helping only when we come to a full stop and can't remember what comes next.

'Dear Jesus, protect Pappa and Mamma, Grandmother and Aunt, Njanjan, Kirsti the kitchen-maid and Murr the cat. May an angel watch over their bedheads and let no evil befall them. Cure Njanjan's rheumatism and let Grandmother sleep from twelve to seven o'clock. Let the boil on Kirsti's foot burst. Also put angels at the bedheads of Uncle Frans, Aunt Sonja, Aunt Leli, Aunt Else, Esja and Goga. May your angels watch over Aunt Luscha, Aunt Laura, Aunt Lotte, Uncle Fabian and fat Uncle Erni. Send even more angels to Uncle Alfred and Aunt Lotte with the black spectacles, Uncle Sus, Uncle Manucha and Aunt Alice – slim Uncle Erni and Aunt Mary and their children, Aunt Ella, Aunt Mausi, Aunt

Olja, Uncle Volodja, Marta, Mika and Ira, good Uncle Georg, Uncle Max and Uncle Karl, Aunt Olga, Aunt Lina and Aunt Helene. Bless the large and the small Aunts Lala, Lady and Meuschen, Uncle Totti and Uncle Bobbi, Aunt Dulla and the lovely Karin – and the Grund aunts in Salmela, Louise, Malla and Gulla. Console Aunt Gulla and let her swollen leg get better and please cure her bad heart. Convert the Papuans to your teachings, so that they are baptized and will be free of sin. Put an end to the war, so that there is peace on earth. Help the wounded soldiers in the trenches and console the poor and sick tonight.

'Dear Jesus, forgive all the sins I have committed today, wash me clean from the dirt of sin and teach me to be a good and obedient child and please Mamma and Pappa. Lean over my bedhead tonight, let Cherubim and Seraphim watch over my bed and keep all evil away from me, so that darkness and sin do not gain foothold in my heart. Amen.'

It's difficult to keep track of all the uncles and aunts and you always forget some names. But it's odd that Grandmother doesn't notice when you leave some of them out, like Uncle Fabian or little Aunt Lala, and allow them to be without an angel to watch over them one night. On the other hand, if you forget Uncle Georg, big Aunt Lala or the Grund aunts, Grandmother corrects you at once and says with a disapproving shake of her head: 'How can you be so careless? Ingratitude is a serious sin.'

Evening prayers end with our saying the Lord's Prayer together with Grandmother. We are talking to God now. God is Jesus' pappa and lives in heaven, but at the same time he is everyone's pappa, Bernt's and mine too. He's just so awfully much bigger and more powerful than our real one. It looks as if even Grandmother is a little afraid of him. She says we have to fear him and you mustn't say his name. Once, when we were playing that Bernt was God and I was the Holy Ghost, Grandmother was really angry and stood us in the corner. God sees and hears everything. He's the one who rolls out the sun in the sky, blows up the storms and downpours and turns day into night. Everything happens on his orders. Everyone has to obey him and he notices at once if anyone is disobedient and doesn't do what he says. So it's quite natural that Grandmother turns to him in the end to put him in a friendly mood, calling down his blessing on the day that has ended and making sure of his help against the evil forces let loose by the coming night. The words she uses to speak to him are obscure and difficult to understand, but her final words – 'For thine is the power and the glory for ever and ever, Amen' – sound so magnificent and tremendous, I feel a shiver running down my spine when I say them. I see the sun rising up to the sky and pouring its dazzling glow all over the world.

When Grandmother has ended her invocation in this way, imprisoning the forces of the night and filling the house to the brim with the forces of good, she says good-night and patters slowly out of the nursery. The darkness soon stands thick outside the window and the house is surrounded by horrible creatures. If Grandmother hadn't said the protective words of the prayers, they would come in and tear us all to pieces.

Up on the slope beyond the kitchen steps, on the other side of the road where the forest begins, there's an outhouse, small and square like a box. Its roof is slanting and covered with black tarpaulin. The outhouse looks stern and gloomy, like an old lady in a black beret. It stands on guard at the frontier of another, secret world, which starts at the edge of the forest and is ruled by other more powerful and more dangerous creatures than people. In the daytime, you usually can't see them and the forest looks perfectly pleasant. But at night the Wolf sits up on the mountain above the outhouse. When I stare out into the darkness, I can see him lying there in the forest, waiting for me. He's almost as big as the mountain itself, black all over like a police dog, with dangling ears, long red tongue and mad, glistening eyes. I know he's thinking about me, that he wants to catch me and eat me up, so I can't get rid of the picture of him.

At night the mountain is also a place for several other evil creatures. They appear as soon as I close my eyes. The Robber lives there with his bearded black face and his long knife, and the Lena beast with an elephant's trunk and streaky hair. The Lena beast usually wears breeches and felt boots and pees huge pools of black water out in the marsh. In the daytime, Porleo, with his hairy, foxy face, stays in the black hole under the stones. He once stole my galosh when Bernt and I climbed over a precipice where a large number of stones were piled on top of each other. Voima also hides under the boulders in the daytime, but I know nothing about her except that she has a black face and white eyes, and that she's the one who sells us milk and paraffin. I found that out once from listening to a conversation between Mamma and Grandmother.

Now they have all assembled down below the nursery window and are staring hungrily up at the window-pane. Sometimes you can hear them whispering and pattering about out there, discussing how they can outwit Grandmother and make their way in without being seen. But all in vain, because an invisible circle has been drawn round the house and none of them can step over it. The actual building is like a transformer, charged with such terrible holy force that everyone who enters it with evil intent suffers immediate death. I don't have to fear anything, the light round the door behind which Grandmother and the other grown-ups are sitting shines so comfortingly. On each side of my bed Seraphim and Cherubim watch over me in their shining white robes and with flaming swords in their hands. Like all angels, they are invisible and I see nothing but darkness when I look for them. But when I close my eyes and press on my eyelids with my fingers, the rainbow-shimmering glitter of their wings appears. And when I'm asleep, several times I have felt their lips fleetingly brushing my forehead.

Grandmother's room is lighter and sunnier than all the others, and it also contains a great many more beautiful and extraordinary things than the other rooms do. But her door is mostly closed and we're never allowed to go in without her calling us herself.

Cinerarias and fuchsias flower on her window-sill and there's a bunch of lilies of the valley in a glass on her bedside table. Above her bed is a pearl embroidery of multicoloured, snakelike entwined letters on a silvery grey background. God himself wrote those letters, which is why they look so strange and why Grandmother has framed them and covered them with glass. For, once upon a time, Grandmother had wrestled with God for a whole night and almost got him down on his back, which is rather amazing considering how small and fragile Grandmother is in comparison with the other grown-ups.

'I shan't let thee go unless thou blesseth me,' Grandmother said to God, and in the end he had to do as she said. As a memorial to the struggle, God sent her the picture with those secret letters on it.

Grandmother always has a wreath of club-moss round the picture. It never withers, and it stays green all winter. But sometimes it begins to look quite messy, and then we have to go out into the forest to look for more club-moss for her.

She has also got a brilliant red feather on her desk. She dips it into the inkwell when she is writing. She was given that by John the Apostle, who pulled it out of the wing of the Angel of the Lord. The desk looks like a castle. It has lots of ledges, colonnades and galleries on three floors on top of each other. It's full of apostles, images of Christ and old photographs. But there are some more amusing things there too – little pale-yellow alpine cows with black necklaces and cowbells, and funny, pop-eyed birds with long, sabre-shaped beaks and moiré plumage, all carved out of wood. Then there's a shimmering amethyst, two dark-eyed cornelians, a petrified sea-urchin and a hollow, amputated hoof in which Grandmother keeps curtain rings, drawing-pins and keys, as well as all kinds of other things. Her most remarkable treasures Grandmother keeps locked in her desk drawer or in her mahogany cupboard. A little white Christ figure sits on the cupboard with his arms outspread. He looks like a pigeon. Grandmother has also got a mirror which is larger than all the other mirrors in the house. When you look into it, you look unclear, as if in a fog, and at the slightest movement your face is distorted and becomes strange and horrible, so you have to turn away in horror.

Grandmother's wash-stand is lined with lead inside and is so heavy only Pappa can move it. Inside it is an invisible pail into which the washing water runs with a gurgling noise. The wash-stand has lots of drawers stuffed with medicine bottles, rolls of oil cloth, enema cans, reddish-brown rubber tubes and other awful things.

In the morning, Mamma knocks on Grandmother's door and we go in to say good-morning to her. She is sitting up in her tall wooden bed, having her tea. In her pale-grey, striped flannel cardigan, she looks even smaller than usual, almost like a child, and has suddenly become like a cat. Her lace cap has gone, and all the rest: her silver hair in thin plaits that remind you of rats' tails and are wound in a wreath round her forehead and temples.

Mamma asks how Grandmother had slept that night, her voice troubled and plaintive, for Grandmother nearly always answers 'Badly!' Sometimes she just says: 'So-so, là là!' Then Mamma at once looks more contented.

It's very strange, this business of Grandmother's sleep, because Grandmother hardly sleeps at all. She says she hasn't slept a wink for decades. And when she does sleep, it's not proper sleep, because she's none the less wide awake and sees everything happening around her. She just lies there with her eyes closed, and she does that for two or perhaps three hours at the most every night. Grandmother also says that human beings can't live with so little sleep, regardless of the fact that she lives all the time as if nothing was wrong with her and she's just as lively and awake in the daytime as the rest of us. But the amazing thing is not just that Grandmother is a mysterious creature who never sleeps and is always wide awake and yet like everyone else, but also that everyone constantly talks about Grandmother's sleep and, every morning, Mamma looks just as horrified when she hears that once again Grandmother has slept for only one or at the most two hours. She starts lamenting, just as if something awful were about to happen. Grandmother herself isn't at all horrified, but just sits there calmly with her cup of tea and listens with a smile.

When Mamma has stopped moaning, we step forward, Grandmother bends down and kisses me on the forehead and then runs her hand lightly over my head. Her kiss is cool and light and smells of dead leaves. When she puts her hand on my head, I feel a peculiar numbness all over me and my knees seem to give way. That's because Grandmother laying on her hands is no ordinary caress, like Mamma's or Pappa's when they put a hand on my head, but a blessing, through which forces of good are invisibly transmitted from her hand to my body.

Although Grandmother is smaller than Pappa, Mamma, Aunt and the other grown-ups, she is the most powerful and distinguished person in our house. No one can measure up to her when it comes to power and wisdom. Everything that happens here at home, even the most insignificant events of our daily life, are an expression of her secret will and wise counsel. But just as God's will doesn't manifest itself when you observe what happens round you, but works invisibly in secret, so does Grandmother's will work so that it is neither seen nor noticed, and you generally think it is the others deciding everything that happens here at home. For Grandmother's strength is not visible in the same way as Pappa's, for instance, when he lifts a cupboard or a gigantic stone, or Aunt's and Mamma's when their eyes flash and their faces turn bright red while you just wait for a smack. Grandmother's strength is like electricity. It can't be seen, but none the less it's always there inside her. You can feel it when you come close to her, and it's a thousand times more dangerous than the strength of all the others put together. It can kill you on the spot if you don't watch out.

Grandmother has this strength because she's old. Not even Uncle Georg or Uncle Frans is as old as she is, although they have snow-white hair and beards. Grandmother is a thousand years old, or perhaps millions. So she knows everything and no one else can compete with her in wisdom, except for God. She doesn't just know everything that's happened since the beginning of the world, she also sees into the future and knows the world will come to an end and what will happen then. She doesn't just know everything happening on earth now at this moment, but also what is happening in heaven and in the underworld. She knows the difference between good and evil, beauty and ugliness, what is permitted and what forbidden. She knows what you have to do for God to like you and let you into heaven, and she knows everything he has forbidden and what you have to watch out for if you want to escape the fires of hell.

Grandmother has seen how God created the world and separated light from dark, how he fixed the sun and the stars in the heavens and filled the earth with all kinds of animals. She tells us about the Garden of Eden, where God used to walk in the evenings. She has still got pictures of Paradise locked in her desk drawer, and sometimes she takes them out and lets us look at them. You can see on them exactly what the Garden looked like with its wonderful fruit trees, thick espaliers of vines and sprouting fountains, strange birds in brilliant colours, blue, red and rain-green, singing in the branches, elephants and leopards strolling along the sandy paths and angels with wreaths of flowers in their hair and zithers in their hands walking slowly past. The play of colours in their slim, pointed wings gives me shivers of ecstasy. Their faces are the most beautiful in the world.

I am particularly fond of a dark-eyed angel with shimmering gold wings, and would like to look for ever at his thin face which always seems slightly sorrowful, despite the magnificence and bliss surrounding him. When I have looked at the picture, I always feel a little unhappy, and everything else that usually amuses me seems dull and meaningless. I've asked Grandmother many a time what his name is and what he is doing with the blue flower he is holding in his hand, but Grandmother doesn't remember him any more and can't tell me anything about him. She says he's not Gabriel nor Michael nor Raphael, for she would recognize them, but one of the minor angels.

In another picture, the Garden of Eden is seething with animals, almost all the animals I know about – lions and tigers, monkeys and crocodiles, flamingos and turtles. And they are all kind to each other. The lion lies pressed up against the side of a rhinoceros, a melon between his paws, and the tiger is licking the roe-deer's neck. The fox is clumsily lolloping about with the hares, and the monkey is trustingly leaning his head against the jackal's chest. Grandmother tells me the animals never ate each other up. They always liked each other so much and wanted to sit as close to each other as possible, and they thought about nothing else except how to help and please each other. The big animals liked the small ones and the strong liked the weak. They all lived off the wonderful refreshing fruits of Paradise, which they picked off the trees and gave to each other.

The evil ones first gained power over creation through the Fall of Man, when the serpent persuaded Eve to eat of the forbidden fruit from the Tree of Knowledge and give it to Adam. The sin they committed was truly terrible, because in that way they were defying God's prohibition, however beautiful the apples on the Tree of Knowledge were. After all, there was plenty of other fruit they could have eaten, oranges and grapes and peaches – not to mention the other kinds of apples which were just as good. Because of their disobedience, they were driven out of Paradise, and Sin and Death have ruled the world ever since. When the animals no longer had access to the lovely fruit and were unable to go on with their happy lives in Paradise, they became cruel and nasty in the same way as people did. They started killing and eating each other. But God put an angel with a flaming sword at the gates of Paradise and ordered the cherubs to pick up the Garden of Eden by its four corners and carry it up to heaven. It freed itself from the ground and floated up above the clouds like a flying carpet. Ever since then, no living creature has been able to find it.

On Sunday mornings, Grandmother reads to us all about love: 'If I spoke in the tongues of people and angels and had no love, then I would be echoing iron or resounding sleigh-bells.'

It's hard to understand, because the words are so strange and Grandmother's voice sounds so peculiar, and it gets more and more difficult to follow, the longer she goes on. You have to sit quite still, and Aunt looks at you now and again to see if you are sitting up straight and have your hands clasped.

The only thing I understand is that love is in your tongue. Mamma has said that love is in your heart and for a while I believed that, but of course Grandmother knows best. Actually, it also sounds quite right when you think about the animals in the Garden of Eden, because it was with their tongues they tasted the fruits they gave each other, and it was with their tongues they licked each other's faces and necks when they wanted to show how much they liked each other, and it was with their tongues they whispered endearments into each other's ears.

Grandmother also says she can speak in many tongues, both of people and angels. Perhaps she has a whole bunch of them in her mouth. Many a time I've tried to look inside Grandmother's mouth to see what angel tongues look like, but she never opens it wide enough. She says only the sound of sleigh-bells would come out of her mouth if she had no love, but then she would also be able to prophesy and move mountains. It worries me rather to think of Grandmother suddenly beginning to jingle like our horse Ahti when he is harnessed to the sleigh, or starting to boom like a church-bell. But the miracle never happens. Grandmother never allows love to run out on its tongues.

'But of faith, hope and love, those three, the greatest of them is love. Amen.'

Grandmother closes the black covers of the Bible and takes off her spectacles, then looks at us with her distant gaze.

'Yes, love is greatest,' sighs Aunt. I notice her eyes are glistening moistly and her nostrils have gone slightly pink. We are allowed to get down from our chairs and run into the nursery.

Love is greater than both faith and hope. But faith must also be very great. Maybe Grandmother means the throne of faith God sits on – and how high is the hop to hope? Is it from here all the way up to heaven – do you then land right in among the angels in Paradise?

Sometimes when the door to Grandmother's room is slightly open, you can see her back as she sits at her desk. She is holding the flaming angel feather in her hand and talking in a low voice to the carved alpine cows and wooden birds, the petrified sea-urchin, the amethyst and the cornelians all lined up on the ledges of her desk. Sometimes she takes one of the apostles or a photograph in her hand, says something to them and then puts them down again. Then she dips the angel feather into the ink and writes for a while so that you can hear the pen scraping against the paper.

When Grandmother goes out, she puts on a tall black hat and ties a silk shawl round it. It covers her chin and mouth so that she looks like a caliph in disguise. She takes a long, walnut-brown walking-stick with an ivory handle and mostly walks about the garden in front of the veranda. She walks round and round the circular sandy path – she seems to have no feet and looks as if she were softly and silently bowling along the ground on invisible rubber wheels. Sometimes she stops in front of a rose-bush or a bed of poppies to speak to some flower or bumble-bee, then she continues her walk. Butterflies and bees dance around her, the flowers bow and sometimes a bird flies down from a tree and twitters plaintively to her.

The sun shines in a particularly mildly subdued way when Grandmother walks round the garden, the air flickering, and from Grandmother comes a golden shimmer like invisible angel wings. For Grandmother has once sat at table with God and the angels outside Abraham's tent in the grove of Mamre. They ate sandwiches, roast veal and cake, and God was very pleased with what was provided.

But although Grandmother is friends with God, so that it's really difficult to distinguish the one from the other, and although she is the oldest, most powerful and wisest person on earth, she also bears a terrible secret that I prefer not to think about. And it's not at all strange that Mamma is so horrified that Grandmother never sleeps at night.

Once – I no longer remember when – I woke up in the middle of the night with a feeling of terror. I had dreamt something awful and, while I was struggling with sleep, I thought I heard voices and the clink of china from the dining-room, where the grown-ups were still up drinking tea. I wanted to rush in to them so that Aunt or Mamma would take me in her arms and protect me from the danger threatening me. But when I looked round our room, I noticed I could just see Aunt's black hair over on the pale-grey square of her pillow. She was breathing heavily and her bare arm was hanging over the edge of the bed like on a dead person. From the opposite corner of the room, where the darkness was thick and black, I could hear Bernt breathing lightly. The room looked much bigger than usual in the grey dawn light trickling in through the window and a veiled murmur of voices was coming from the dining-room. Some of them were still in there, but their voices didn't sound human. Some of them were sitting in there whispering, slobbering and grunting in a peculiar way. The light round the door was a fiery blood-red. I crept silently over to the door and put my eye to the keyhole.

What a sight! A company of ghosts and spectres sitting in a circle round the festive dining-room table with its innumerable lighted candles. Grandmother was sitting right in the middle of the guests! On her right was a monster with a horse's face and on her left a ghost in a black hood pulled over his head like a sack. There they were, the Wolf and the Robber, the Lena beast and Porleo, Voima and Krabbarak the magician, and all the others I'm afraid of, all the ghosts with black faces and grinning white teeth, skeletons and will-o'-the-wisps.

Grandmother is good friends with them all. She is nodding right and left, smiling and pressing them to help themselves. The dishes go round, the candle-flames flutter, and the monsters grab with hairy paws and white spidery fingers, grubbing and sucking at bones they then crunch between their teeth. Then they lick their lips with satisfaction. Suddenly I see Grandmother leaning over her plate and putting something up to her mouth with her fingers. It's the amputated hand of a child – I can see the chubby fold at the wrist and the little pink fingers sticking out from the back of the hand. Grandmother bites into the hand, ripping and tearing off long strips of skin and flesh, gnawing at the hand as if it were a chicken bone, then neatly lining up the shiny white bones on the edge of her plate. Her temples and ears move up and down as she chews, and gravy runs thickly out of the corners of her mouth, but she doesn't even bother to wipe it away with her table-napkin.

12

THERE ARE THREE CREATURES WHOSE NAMES NO ONE MAY say out aloud. They are called the Devil, Satan and Beelzebub. Grandmother has forbidden us to say their names. She says it's a great sin to do so.

Sin is something so horrible and awful you have to watch out for it in every possible way. Sin is like a big black patch – like when you've done bigs in your trousers – and you have to keep a constant watch over yourself so that you don't commit a sin by mistake, for then God gets dreadfully angry and punishes you. It's very difficult to avoid sin, in fact impossible, because you can't see it and so often you don't know when you've sinned. Only Grandmother understands how to find the black patch on your soul.

Pappa, Uncle Georg, Uncle Max and the other uncles also sin sometimes. When they get really angry and their faces turn as red as a turkeycock, they yell and call on those three evil creatures. It looks to me as if the uncles weren't at all afraid to do so – both the thin and the fat Uncle Erni are always doing it, even when they aren't at all angry. Perhaps God doesn't dare punish them because they are so big and strong.

The Devil, Satan and Beelzebub are different creatures. There is, of course, some obscure connection between them. When I think about any of them, their names are also on the tip of my tongue. They must be three friends who are different in appearance and temperament, but they always stick together. It took me a long time before I got to know the characters hiding behind those awful and dangerous words.

One day an aunt in a salmon-pink silk blouse, with lots of wavy hair and a lorgnette dangling on her bosom, came from St Petersburg. She brought with her the Devil enclosed in a glass tube and gave it to me.

When you pressed the rubber covering that closed the mouth of the tube, the Devil leapt up and down in the tube like a little frog. I was delighted and found the Devil very nice and neat, hardly bigger than a bumble-bee as he stood there in the transparent tube, staring at me with his white eyes. His tubby, dark-brown body shone with a secretive dark light, like a semitransparent kind of stone, and the horns on his head were thin and curved like a snail's. I showed everyone the way the Devil silently floated upwards in the tube and always smiled at you with the same rigid white smile.

I carried the tube with me everywhere, and at night fell asleep with it beside me on the bedside table, knowing full well I needed only to stretch out my hand to reach the Devil. In comparison with him, all my other toys were dull, apparently tarnished and sullen, with neither life nor the ability to move. Floating upwards in a vacuum, overcoming gravity and flying without wings – that was real magic, of which only the Devil was capable.

But after a while I began to feel sorry for the Devil in his transparent prison. He kept begging me to free him –

then he would fly up high and fetch a star down for me from the sky.

Hitherto I had held only the Starfish and the Star of Bethlehem in my hand. Grandmother keeps the Starfish locked in her desk drawer. It's like a ginger biscuit, so you feel like eating it. The Star of Bethlehem, which is fastened to the very top of the Christmas tree, confuses your eye with its sparkling shimmer. It's ruffled like a bird and prickles you with its rough, glistening, golden brush. But although those things are wonderful, the stars at night in their millions gathering in the sky above our house are even more wonderful. Sometimes I see one of them falling down like white lightning on the edge of the forest near our home. I've asked several times to be allowed to run out into the forest to look for the star, but I've never been allowed to.

When it had grown dark, I crept out on to the veranda with the tube in my hand. Through the tall windows I could just make out the dark tree-tops like bell-towers and above them the sky, festively decorated like a pearly pattern on blue velvet. That evening, the stars were wonderfully large and sparkling like a swarm of firebirds. I climbed on to a bench and opened the window, all ready to release the Devil and let him fly out into the darkness. He would pick me some stars and come flying back with them through the window. Then I would shut them in a cardboard box and feed them with breadcrumbs. Once I possessed this wonderful treasure, I would be able to conjure up anything I wished for in a moment.

At first I tried to open the tube by pressing hard on the rubber skin on the top. Even the lightest of pressure was enough to make the Devil float up to the top of the tube. But by pressing harder, I could give him the strength to burst the tube and soar off into space.

It was so dark I could hardly distinguish what was going on inside the tube I was holding up in the air. But although I pressed hard, the tube held and the Devil could still just be seen humiliatingly squashed at the top. Then I squeezed the tube hard with both hands. I don't know how it happened, but I crushed the glass easily between my fingers. Something cold and wet ran over my hands down on to the window-sill I was leaning on. I couldn't see whether the Devil swung himself out of the window. It was so dark I could hardly make out anything at all, and I very soon felt a stinging pain in the palms of my hands, as if they had been round some glowing object. Terrified, I rushed into the dining-room, where they were all sitting round the lamp. When I looked at my hands, they were covered with blood.

The grown-ups took charge of me. It was perfectly obvious they were displeased, but I was much too frightened to bother about that. Passively, I allowed myself to be taken to Grandmother's room, where I had to stand with my hands over a wash-bowl. Drops of blood fell into the water and grew into scarlet clouds. Although Grandmother kept dabbing my hands with cotton wool, the red juice kept coming out of the cuts in my hands again as if out of a sponge. Then I had to endure even worse suffering. With a sewing needle, Grandmother poked about in the cuts to get out the pieces of glass. Then she took the iodine bottle, dipped a wad of cotton wool in the brown liquid and pressed it against the wounds. My hands were covered with dark-brown, rusty patches. It stung as if she had set fire to my hands. I couldn't hold back any longer and began to howl.

The next morning when I went out on to the veranda with my hands and fingers wrapped up in thick white gauze bandages, I had almost forgotten the Devil and his night-time flight to the stars. My experiences in Grandmother's room had been far too upsetting. But when I went over to the table, I found the Devil in an ashtray among broken matches and cigarette-ends. He was lying on his back, showing his curved, tortoise-brown stomach. One horn was broken off and he looked deplorably like a dried-up dead beetle, but he was still staring ahead with the same rigid white smile. I took him out of the ashtray and held him between my fingers, which the bandages had made clumsy and numb. But there was no doubt about it. He was dead. He could neither fly nor leap nor keep himself floating in the air. There was no magic about him at all any longer and I don't know what happened to him after that.

Kirsti told me later that she had found him under the bench when she had swept the veranda in the morning, just by the window in front of which I had broken the glass tube. What had happened on his night journey through the multitude of stars has remained a secret. Anyhow, his fate was sealed at dawn as the veranda wall glowed peacefully in the pink morning light.

For a long, long time I knew nothing about Satan. Whenever I pronounced his nasty, hissing, somehow grey-bearded name, I saw no picture in front of me. He lacked face, voice and shape. And yet I could hear from the very ring of his name that he was the nastiest and most dangerous of all those three creatures who belonged together.

But finally he appeared to me in a dream.

I am walking in the garden in front of the veranda. The sun is burning down on the raked sandy paths, the flowers glowing gaudily and brightly. I look at the violet helmets of the aconites, the bumble-bees buzzing all round them, and I lean over the fiery red bowls of the poppies powdered with violet pollen. The peonies are swelling like great balls of satin, the delphiniums raising their pointed hats above my head and looking at me with close clusters of black eyes.

Suddenly a shadow seems to sweep over the garden, although there isn't a cloud in the sky. The light takes on an ashen tinge and the flowers and grass turn pale. Someone is standing there in the garden – invisibly.

Terrified, I look for him behind bushes and between hedges, but there's nothing there except flowers and the lawn. The more I search, the more eager I become, and my terror of quite unexpectedly catching sight of him makes my heart thump harder and harder.

Then all at once, as I approach the berberis-bush, he glides out from behind it like a dark shadow. I scream with terror and rush away. I flee through the garden, past the veranda to the kitchen steps and try to open the door to get inside. But the door is locked. All the doors in the house are locked. Three times I run round the house. When I look back, I can't see anything, but I know I am being followed and my terror grows each time round.

As I turn the corner between the veranda steps and the kitchen balcony for the third time, and come to the privy window with its ragged lace curtain, Satan rushes out from round the corner of the house. He's hardly bigger than a puppy, black all over, with insane, glowing white eyes and a red tongue that flaps like a fiery flame in his mouth. He barks so terribly and horribly that the trees, the ground and the sky start back at every bark, as if struck by lightning. Although I run away as fast as I can, he catches up with me, snapping at my bare legs. I scream so loudly, I wake up.

I've never got to know Beelzebub as well as I have the Devil and Satan. He always stays on the very edge of my existence, where he is glimpsed as something pale and gangling. He is not so evil as the Devil and Satan, so is not so interesting as they are. In actual fact, Beelzebub is none other than Uncle Fabian.

Uncle Fabian is almost always away, and when he comes to Teerilä he stays hidden in Aunt Luscha's shabby grey old house. Just as everywhere else, this house is ruled over by a female trinity, Aunt Luscha, Aunt Lotte and Aunt Laura.

Aunt Luscha is the eldest, the most powerful and the wisest. She has silver-grey hair and the tired mouth of an old lioness. She is holy and good because she is friends with Grandmother and often visits her in her room to talk about holy things. She was married to old Uncle Bill, who now lies buried over in the churchyard. Old Uncle Bill wasn't a person but an ape from Africa who moved out of the primeval jungle and became a priest and married Aunt Luscha. He must have looked terrible, black and hairy all over as he was. They say he was also a man-eater.

When Aunt Luscha is on a visit to Grandmother, the door into Grandmother's room is always closed so that no one hears the perfectly dreadful things Aunt Luscha talks about with Grandmother. If you creep up to the door and put your ear to the keyhole, you hear nothing but 'Oh yes, yes, Luscha dear!' or 'No, no, Muscha dear!' And then there's a tittling and tattling no one can possibly make head or tail of.

Later, after Aunt Luscha has gone, Mamma and Grandmother always speak French, occasionally giving us annoyed sideways looks and telling us to hurry up with our milk and sandwiches. Mamma speaks very loudly and her face looks angry, then dismayed and horrified. The names Lotte, Laura and Fabian constantly crop up between the mysterious foreign words. Grandmother is calm as always, listening and just saying now and again: 'Tout à fait, tout à fait.'

Next in rank to Aunt Luscha comes Aunt Lotte, although she's younger than Aunt Laura, but she is seen and talks much more than her sister. She's the ordinary Aunt Lotte, as opposed to the Aunt Lotte with dark glasses – the one who lives in Uncle Alfred's house down by the lake.

The ordinary Aunt Lotte has great big glistening roe-deer eyes that roll round in her head like black marbles, and she has a wide mouth like a frog's. She tells horrible stories. Once she invited Bernt and me home and told us the story of Stromian the dog, and right in the middle of the story she turned herself into a dog and scuttled round the floor, barking so horribly I started crying. But Aunt Lotte only occasionally lives turned into a dog running round outside Aunt Luscha's house barking so that you daren't walk past. Sometimes she turns herself into a man, so she can visit other men and cheat them into friendship. Then she frightens them by turning herself into Stromian the dog. The terrified men have several times taken a gun and fired at that horrible dog, but Aunt Lotte is the kind no one can kill. After a while she visits them in the form of a handsome foreign youth.

Aunt Laura hardly ever comes to see us, and when she does, she is always with Aunt Lotte. Her clothes are much more stylish and grander than those of all the other aunts. She wears colourful silk scarves round her neck or round her head like a gypsy. Everything of Aunt Laura's is beautiful, her forehead, her nostrils, the line of her chin and throat and her fingertips. The material of her dresses is light and thin, creeping like lizard-skin round her waist and letting all the movements of her body show underneath. When she walks or stands, her long, slim legs can just be seen through the material. No other aunt emanates such a gentle, mysterious fragrance of flowers as Aunt Laura. Just because of this fragrance, you always want to be near her, and preferably to sit on her lap. It is lovely to stroke the cool, smooth material of her dress and feel mysterious buckles and buttons underneath it. But Aunt Laura doesn't like you sitting on her lap, because then you crease her dress. She doesn't take much notice of you, in fact hardly even notices whether you are in the room.

Sometimes Aunt Laura plucks on a guitar and sings, which is really beautiful. All the grown-ups sit in silence, although some of them do look rather sleepy, and now and again she takes out a cigarette, rolls it between her rosy-pink pointed fingertips and lights it just like a man. Perhaps this is what frightens Grandmother and Mamma most of all, and shows how dangerous Aunt Laura actually is. Sometimes Aunt Laura sings a song about how she used to sit on a rock with her hair down and bewitch passing fishermen with her singing and playing, so that their boats ran aground and they were drowned in the waves.

But if Aunt Lotte and Aunt Laura are dangerous, Grandmother and Mamma are still much more afraid of Uncle Fabian. Grandmother always purses her mouth a little when she says Uncle Fabian's name, as if the name itself tasted nasty. Everything bad and dangerous in Aunt Luscha's house comes in the end from Uncle Fabian. We're never allowed in Aunt Luscha's house when he is there. Mamma says that could cost us our lives.

Aunt let us go with her one day to Aunt Luscha's house when she had a message to take there. Afterwards Mamma scolded her so fiercely, both of them turned red in the face, and then Aunt went and sat in the nursery and cried with her face in her hands. Yet all we had done was to stand in the hall for a short time while Aunt spoke to Aunt Luscha, and we hadn't seen anything of Uncle Fabian.

One day I was sitting on Mamma's lap on the veranda, having toast and hot milk, when suddenly a tall, gangling man I'd never seen before came through the door. He was wearing a pale-grey dotted suit with a dark-red bow-tie, and he had a pair of light-yellow gloves in his hand. He was in every way much more stylish than any of the other uncles I had got to know.

At first Mamma seemed slightly frightened. She quickly put down the cup of milk I hadn't had time to finish and pushed me down off her knee. They greeted each other without shaking hands, the uncle elegantly swinging his arm out, putting his hand on his heart and bowing deeply. Mamma's hands fumbled with my bib strings and her face turned scarlet. She asked him to sit down, then, running her hand over my head in passing, she told me to go out into the garden. Her expression was very friendly then, as if she were delighted with the visit, her eyes never leaving the uncle as he sat down at the table opposite us. With a smile, she asked him how he was.

'I haven't finished,' I said, offended.

'You can drink your milk later. . . .' Mamma's voice sounded impatient. 'Or . . . listen to me now, take your toast and cup and go into the kitchen. I expect Aunt is there.'

I didn't in the least want to go, because I was curious about this new uncle. I very much wanted him to notice me and say something, so we could get to know each other and I could get up on his lap. Reluctantly, I took my milk and half-eaten toast and set off towards the door, dragging my feet on purpose, and when I was behind Mamma's back, I stopped to look. Maybe she would forget me and let me stay, for they did seem to be absorbed in their conversation.

The new uncle had dark hair brushed straight back and a sharp, thin face. His eyebrows divided away from the top of his nose and then ran upwards towards his temples. His thin neck was stretched forward so that his chin and lower lip shot out in a haughty, superior expression. Mamma was doing all the talking. He said nothing.

For a moment he looked at me as if expecting something, and I saw the skin over his cheekbones was stretched tight and trembling slightly. But he said nothing. When he later shook the ash off his cigarette and lit a match, the movements were strangely slippery and gliding, like a shadow.

Mamma suddenly turned round, got up and came over to me. 'Out you go, now! Immediately!' she said, giving me a shove and making the milk spill on to my trousers and stockings.

'Look what you've done! You've spilt my milk,' I cried indignantly.

Mamma roughly took hold of my arm and leant down so that we were face to face. Hers was very pale. 'Now do as you're told!' she whispered, and squeezed my arm so hard it felt as if she had bitten me.

This new humiliation disconcerted me completely

and I started howling at the top of my voice, Mamma, the stranger uncle, the whole veranda dissolving into shimmering circles of light from my tears. Suddenly I was in the kitchen and Njanjan and Aunt were there. Mamma shook me. I tried to get free to go back to the veranda.

'You pinched me! You pinched me!' I bawled as loudly as I could, so that Aunt and Njanjan would know how nasty Mamma was. 'I don't want to stay in the kitchen. I want to see the new uncle.'

Mamma had never been so nasty before. She looked awful, her eyes flashing, her hair in disorder, her lips pressed together and stretched across her jaw like on a monster. Her face and neck were all trembling wrinkles and sinews that had never been there before, and they made her look more horrible than ever.

'Don't you understand, you stupid child? It's Uncle Fabian!'

I was so terrified I stopped crying. I don't know which was worse, Mamma's face or that she had said Uncle Fabian's name out aloud.

'Take him,' Mamma went on after a while to Aunt. 'And make sure he doesn't set foot on the veranda. See to it that the other children keep away too. I must go back to him now.'

Afterwards, after Uncle Fabian had vanished and I was allowed out of the kitchen, Mamma was washing her hands at the wash-stand in Grandmother's room. The door was open and she was talking excitedly to Grandmother.

'You must tell Aunt Luscha she should forbid him to show himself here. There are small children here!'

'Come over here!' she called as soon as she caught sight of me. 'You must wash your hands too. Did you touch the chair, or anything else Uncle Fabian had touched? . . . No, not this water. We must change the water and clean the bowl first. Heavens, now you've gone and put your hands in it! Just when I'd told you. . .!

Such disobedient children simply drive one mad!'

We weren't allowed back on the veranda until after dinner, and the chair Uncle Fabian had been sitting on had been moved out into the porch. We had to promise Mamma that we would never sit on it or touch it again.

It's taken a long time to fathom out the secret about Uncle Fabian, but now I understand what happened on the veranda.

In secret, with Bernt, I've looked in a book Pappa has on his shelf and in it are pictures of Beelzebub. And Beelzebub has a face exactly like Uncle Fabian's when he visits people. Actually, it's unimportant that I didn't see any horns on Uncle Fabian's forehead or notice the hoofs right through his brown shoes. You can see it on his face, and Uncle Fabian has the face of Beelzebub, or Beelzebub has Uncle Fabian's face – it doesn't matter which. Anyhow, he may well have drawn in his horns like a snail, then brushed his hair over the tips so that they didn't show. I didn't have time to see how he behaved out there on the veranda. He also limped a little as he came through the door and went over to Mamma, as if one of his shoes didn't fit properly. And Beelzebub has exactly the same habit of calmly crossing his legs when he sits down, jutting his chin out and inclining his head slightly with a polite but at the same time amused smile, to listen to what is being said to him.

But then there's an even more horrible thing.

Uncle Fabian hasn't got ordinary foamy white spit, but bright-red blood in his mouth. He goes round spitting blood. Mamma is frightened he'll spit on us, because if he does we'll drop dead on the spot. The blood kills more surely than a snake-bite, and if one single drop of it sticks to your clothes or skin, you drop down and give up the ghost.

That's why Mamma was so terrified when Uncle Fabian came to visit us. She knew he had come to spit on us. And I didn't even realize it was Uncle Fabian, but just stood there quite unaware of the danger threatening me and I didn't want to go away. Supposing Uncle Fabian had spat on me the moment he came in, or when I was standing behind Mamma's chair looking at him! I shouldn't have had time to duck or squat down. The stream of red blood would have shot out of his mouth like lightning and hit me in the heart. Of course his friendly manner was just his cunning disguise. Now, afterwards, I remember he kept moistening his lips and measuring the distance to where I was standing, his tongue playing in his mouth as he spoke and sliding out between his lips several times. It looked like a sting and the tip was forked like on a snake. All the time Uncle Fabian's face never moved, like a toad's, but his jaw muscles and cheeks trembled when he drew them tight to suck his mouth properly full of blood.

Uncle Fabian is not only dangerous because he spits blood. He's also dangerous because he has got only one lung. He has coughed up the other one, Mamma says, and from her voice and expression I can see that that's even more dangerous than spitting blood. His chest is quite hollow on one side, where there's nothing but darkness and emptiness, as in a tomb. Uncle Fabian has coughed up the lung that was inside there and blown it out of his mouth, so that it sailed away through the air like a great red balloon. Nowadays Uncle Fabian breathes with only one lung, like a snake. Since then his breath has become so dangerous he needs to blow only a little bit for you to turn to ice. His breath is colder than a ghost's or an evil spirit's, because it comes from that black empty space in his chest.

Nowadays I think with horror about once wanting to climb up on to Uncle Fabian's lap. Everything he has breathed on becomes bewitched and dangerous, so you mustn't touch it. Every time I walk past the veranda chair in the porch, I shudder as I feel the chill still coming out of it.

13

THE VAST EXPANSE OF THE UNKNOWN WORLD STARTS ON the opposite shore of the great wide lake down below the park round the Big House. I often sit on the Big House veranda steps looking over towards the horizon fading into blue across the lake. The steps are high and wide like church steps and slowly descend towards the cool, shadowy park, its secretive, leafy paths and impenetrable hedges of acacia and spiraea. The steps are of grey, unpainted wood, and you can spread your toys out on them as on a floor. From down in the park the steps look as if they lead up into the clouds. They're the staircase up to heaven Jacob saw in his dream, the angels standing on each side of it and God the Father himself at the top radiating a gentle, moonlike glow.

Up on the veranda, with its dignified white pillars and the curved rail that reminds me of sugar icing, Uncle Frans sits leaning back in a folding chair, his silver-topped walking-stick in his hand. He wears a black slouch hat and has a striped rug across his knees. His white beard spreads impressively all over his chest, running from one ear to the other like a sea captain's. His eyes are small and almost hidden by baggy folds of skin covering the outer corners of his eyes and giving his face a gentle, weary, all-knowing look. Uncle Frans is dressed either in a white jacket and black waistcoat or a black jacket and white waistcoat. I don't understand why he can never dress all in white or all in black. That would be both more orderly and more beautiful.

Sometimes when I'm playing on the floor beside him, he stretches out his stick and hooks the silver handle round the back of my knee. It doesn't make any difference if I wriggle and try to get free. He pulls me to him like a fisherman hauling in his line with a fish wriggling on the end of it. But Uncle Frans isn't at all dangerous and I actually rather like being caught in this way. His beard is soft and woolly like the fur of a ram and it feels nice to have his arm round my waist and listen to his quiet, purring voice. He raises his stick with his other hand, aims the black ferrule at the wavy, bluish horizon and pronounces unknown and strangely high-sounding names.

I stand leaning against Uncle Frans and stare out at that secretive world I've never yet been to and which is full of the most amazing and remarkable things. Uncle Frans is almost as old as Grandmother and almost as wise as she is. He knows everything about the world. You can see it from his veranda and he can tell you about it. Nothing I have seen so far is as amazing as the mountains Uncle Frans talks about. They are hidden in dark cloaks and squat down far away in a semicircle round the world, where earth and sky merge together and the world itself comes to an end.

The Kukkarovuori is the shape of a half-moon and looks dark and dismal. But inside its black interior are endless hidden treasures, the whole mountain full of gold, silver and copper coins, amethysts, sapphires, rubies and other glittering jewels. The Karhuvuori is even more dismal and dark and is inhabited by a horde of black bears which tear you to pieces as soon as you try to step on to it. Behind the Kukkarovuori the St Hubertus shoots up its hump, its back running to the right in a jagged, wavy, sinking line. The St Hubertus is actually higher than the Kukkarovuori, although it looks lower, because, like a snail, it has crept down and hidden itself behind the Kukkarovuori. A single curved spire shoots up into the sky out of its hump – sometimes it isn't a spire but a glittering cross. The St Hubertus is holy. Inside it, enchanted knights, pious hermits and white deer with silver crosses between their horns all live their secret lives.

Most of all, though, I like the Kuningasvuori. Its bare back glitters like a sand dune. Sometimes, when it's hot, you can see little bluish figures moving on its peak, dancing on their own, floating in the air, suspended for hours above the flickering contours of the mountain. In the evenings, the mountain frees itself from the earth so that a streak of white space appears between it and the horizon. It's like seeing a coral island with a few palms on it floating in the air. When twilight falls or it clouds over before it starts raining, the Kuningasvuori conjures itself away – you see nothing but a glimpse of a shadow-like contour of forest in the place where the mountain usually is.

14

'IT'S SUCH LOVELY WEATHER TODAY,' SAYS GRANDMOTHER after breakfast. 'Supposing we go to Salmela and visit the Grund aunts?'

Aunt gets out newly ironed white blouses for Bernt and me, and I have put on my blue-and-white striped socks and my new sandals. We put white summer hats on our heads, Aunt pats our cheeks and we're ready to go.

At first we fetch the oars and rowlocks from the Big House, then we walk in single file through the flickering, leafy tunnel down to the lake. Mamma opens the creaking, grey gate – it's difficult to get through it, because suddenly the oar I'm carrying swings round and bars our way like a boom. But then Uncle Georg helps me and we suddenly find ourselves out in the light and the smell of mud from the lake reaches our noses.

The shore is muddy and wet, but a walkway of stones leads to the jetty, on each side of it alder-bushes with their sticky leaves, horrid holes eaten in them by jewel-like beetles. You have to walk carefully so as not to slip on the glistening cowpats. A big, mottled cow blocks our way several times. Uncle Georg yells at it to get out of the way, but it just turns its back and contemptuously slaps its tail at us. We have to wait for a long while before it disappears into the alder-bushes with an ungainly leap.

The ground on both sides of the high walkway is covered with old rushes that have faded in the sun and look like woven rattan. A little way below is dark-brown water, where the cows stand up to their knees, their white bellies reflected in the water. They look dully at us, munching away all the time and mumbling something incomprehensible to themselves. Then comes a flickering carpet of horizontally striped horse-tail stems. They're hollow and I can take them apart like pieces of a machine – little poles with a forklike wreath of black spikes at the end. They're thin and slender and make me think of music. After that, masses of tall, rustling reeds with brown, feathery tufts on top and knifelike leaves that cut your fingers if you try to pull them up. Lumps of slimy green mud remind you of snot, great bubbles staring at me like tummy buttons. A few yellow water-lilies lift their shining, tightly closed buds from the black water.

We come out on to the jetty. The planks sag under our weight with long, echoing cries. The boats are tied up on each side of the jetty, slowly rising and falling and now and again dragging sleepily on their rusty mooring-chains.

The workers' boats are long and black, shiny with sticky tar. The uncles' are broad and heavy, painted in bright colours, white, blue and red. Our own boat is yellow, but for some reason is always at the bottom of the lake like a shipwreck. So we choose Uncle Georg's boat.

It's as high and heavy as a venerable old family bed.

'Are you sure it doesn't leak, Georg?' says Grandmother. 'Last year when we took your boat, my feet got wet and we had to turn back before we'd even got out on the lake.'

'Must have been rainwater,' snorts Uncle Georg. 'It poured all last summer. Anyhow, I've had it painted and tarred again. You needn't worry.'

'I suppose we've got everything? The basket with the mineral water and my heart medicine,' says Grandmother. 'Give me my parasol, Anni, the sun's blazing down terribly. And where's my umbrella? It looks as if it'll rain any minute now.'

It takes quite a while before Uncle Georg has undone the endlessly rattling chain wound round the jetty piles in cunningly tangled coils and we have all managed to stow ourselves on board. When Grandmother has sat down beside Uncle Georg astern and put up her parasol, she notices she has forgotten to bring her book and her glasses with her, so Aunt has to run back home for them.

At last everything is ready. Mamma sits down at the oars, Aunt pushes the boat out and we slowly glide away from the jetty. I curl up in the prow. First come algae and water-lily leaves – little silvery, shiny beetles quickly fly off them as we approach. Then sun dances like a fragment of mirror on the rippling water and I can see the shadow of my own head and the prow of the boat like the toe of a shoe. When I hang my head over the edge of the boat, I can see the little silvery white waves round the keel, gurgling and rippling like a spring. I quickly reach out and pull up a water-lily as it glides past. It's like a white star with curly filigree work in the middle, trembling drops of water rolling round inside it like crystal balls. Its scent is sweet and acrid at the same time. It reminds me of marzipan and water-melons. I hold on to the long stem and let the flower drag along the water. A plough-shaped pattern of glittering ruffles glides behind us.

We are still in the channel leading through the belt of reeds out towards the bay, the dark surface of the water covered with white water-lilies and a forest of rushes rising on each side of us. When the boat gets too close to the rushes, it rustles and roars all around us as if a gale were about to blow up. The stems of the rushes glide softly and submissively aside, then rise again, trembling and shaking their brown heads as soon as the boat has slid past. I bend over and pull at a rush stem. It's awfully long, and when I hold it upright it seems taller than fat Uncle Erni and Uncle Manucha, the tallest and largest of all the uncles. And I'm very proud of having such a long rush. Its bottom end is white and fragile as if it were made of sugar. I bite off a little bit and put it in my mouth. But it just tastes slightly of marshy water and grass.

As soon as we've come out of the channel, the waves splash excitedly against the bottom of the boat. I hear someone drumming against it with their fingers, and laughing. Far away I can see the jetty, the shore and the grazing cows, and the Big House rising out of the dark foliage of the park. Everything has suddenly grown foolishly small. Only the oaks in the park have grown and spread themselves out, hiding the horizon with their cloudlike tops.

The lake now reminds me of a wide river. We row past the ferry, which slowly slides along its steel cable stretched tight like a bowstring under the pressure. Some peasant women in black headcloths are on deck with a horse and cart. A man turns a big red wheel and the steel cable rolls itself up. It's like looking at toys on a tray.

After the ferry comes a long yellow house with ornate window-sills and eaves that look like lace.

'Look, Georg!' says Grandmother. 'There's General Grund's old villa. How time passes, and how everything changes!' The house is in the middle of a big garden full of apple trees which fill me with secret longing and envy. Children are running about playing on the dead-straight sandy paths, and in their colourful clothes they look like butterflies. Once upon a time – it must have been just after the creation of the World – when Aunt Louise and her sisters were as small as we are now, they lived in that old yellow house with their father, General Grund. He had forty horses and rode in a carriage.

When I close my eyes, I can see the general in front of me. He looks forbidding and has a long beard like God the Father himself. His coat is red and flashes with gold and silver, and he has a scimitar. The forty horses tumble round his carriage as the general gallops down to the ferry. The black leather hood of the carriage bobs up and down and behind the general are Aunt Louise, Aunt Malla and Aunt Gulla. Actually, they look just as they do today, old and wrinkled, with silver-grey hair, but they are as small as little old dwarfs and have long pigtails like whips sticking out from the backs of their heads. Each one of them has a little red apple in her hand and is munching it. I don't really know how the general's forty horses manage to find room on the ferry. The general, the galloping horses and the midget aunts disappear like a whirlwind through the darkening space, like the prophet Elijah when he ascended to heaven.

The landscape around us becomes more and more dreamlike. The boat floats silently through the bright space, the stones on the shore, the reeds, the trees, the jetties and the light summer villas slowly appearing out of the dark contours of the shore and then gliding back into it. Wonderful fairy-like women live there, their mysteriously secretive names – Schwanebach, Else Delevron – caressing your ears like music. Their pavilions of brown, carved wood stand on the shore like little Chinese pagodas, reflecting their pointed roofs.

'Poor Else Delevron!' says Mamma, holding the oar blade high in the air.

'Yes, poor Else Delevron,' repeats Grandmother thoughtfully.

'To think what she's been through,' says Mamma, taking another stroke. 'That cruel husband and her little deaf-mute son. . . .'

Else Delevron's pavilion is on a little skerry out in the lake. A long, narrow bridge arches over the water, so delicate it would collapse at once if anyone with a more worldly name dared to step on to it. Its windows of multicoloured glass and the pavilion flash in the sunlight like a Japanese lantern.

From Mamma's and Grandmother's softly spoken conversation I realize that Else Delevron is deeply unhappy. Her husband is very nasty and has gone far away, and somehow or other it is his fault that his son is deaf and dumb. Maybe the boy was born without ears or tongue, or had the husband one night secretly cut them off and then run away? Else Delevron has had that wonderful pavilion built to console the poor boy. When he sits inside it and looks at the world through the multicoloured glass panes, everything is so beautiful he forgets he can never talk to anyone or tell them how lonely and sad he is.

The Misses Schwanebach's pavilion is behind the next headland and you can just see a young woman in dark clothes inside it. She is sitting reading, her elbow propped up on the pavilion railing. As we glide past, she doesn't even raise her head. I feel quite melancholy and solemn. She is so wonderfully beautiful, so inaccessible and solitary, her white dress airy and as light as swan's-down. She is sitting there waiting for night to fall, then she will turn into a bird and fly across the lake in the form of a swan.

The last pavilion is on the furthest headland of Oravansaari, high up on a gigantic cliff rising out of the water, a steep stairway leading up to it. Like a suspension bridge, it hovers between the shore rocks and the rock which is shaped like an upright egg. The golden brown contours of the upside-down pavilion glisten, oily and slippery, in the dark water. The pavilion is always empty, the gulls stepping uneasily about on the balustrade, then lifting their wings with sorrowful and dismal cries. Rust-coloured streaks like blood run down the cliff's bulging surface; the closer we get, the more hollow become the sound of the waves and the splash of the oars. Sometimes I think I can make out the distant echo of a harp.

Beyond the faded, lilac-coloured surface of the lake, I can just see the marshy meadows of Vendelä. The wind is brisk and the water winks from innumerable silvery, shimmering scales. I can see the cowshed, the farm-workers' cottages and the tall, leafy oaks hiding the main house. Behind them is the mountain range framing the view from the veranda of the Big House. But now the mountains are closer and look much darker and more menacing, as if they were annoyed at our coming so close to them, and I am slightly afraid.

'I have a message for General Derleff,' says Mamma. 'Supposing we tie up at his jetty so that I could look in on him. Do you want to come too, children?'

The house where the general lives looks like a palace, with tall white pillars and two marble lions guarding the steps on either side. They have large white balls between their paws. The pillars, the lions and the actual steps are all as blindingly white as snow. I've never before seen anything so magnificent and beautiful, and it seems both inappropriate and dangerous to force your way in there.

But Mamma doesn't seem to realize that. She opens the iron gate and, when there is no one in sight in the garden, she fearlessly goes up the steps and disappears into the house. But I daren't and stay outside on the raked path between rows of flaring red and blue flowers. At a distance I admire the lions crouching on the steps with flapping manes and wide-open jaws. They look at me with contempt and frown heavily, as if urging me to go away as quickly as possible.

Supposing they suddenly came alive and leapt down from the steps! Don Juan was visited by a stone idol which despite all his protests dragged him down to hell with him. And that happened on our very own veranda! In the middle of the night. I heard the marble statue's horrible knocking on the veranda door as well as the stir it caused. The tinkle of glass, the whimpering and the Commodore's terrible stamping making the whole house shake. The light penetrating right out into the garden and glimmering gloomily in the spruce-needles outside the nursery window suddenly went out and it was pitch dark all round me. Hell opened its mouth and I heard Satan's mocking laughter. It sounded hollow, as if coming from a barrel.

While I'm standing looking at the lions thinking about all this, a tall uncle suddenly appears with Mamma and Bernt. He is so terribly tall I can see only his shiny new pigskin shoes and pale-grey flannel trousers.

'Why didn't you bow? It's the general himself,' Bernt whispers.

But I don't really trust him. Generals usually wear quite different clothes. The real general is sure to be staying hidden in the house. While Mamma sits down in a basket chair on the terrace and talks to the false general, I go across to look at the lions.

The strange thing is that they are real lions from whatever direction you look at them. They look perfectly alive, lifting their paws, swinging their tails and opening their mouths so wide their tongues stick out, as if they want to frighten anyone who comes anywhere near them. There's something lovely and dignified about them. In the end, I pluck up my courage and cautiously touch one of the paws. It feels strangely cold and hard. Soon I'm no longer afraid. I let my hands run over the lion's back and feel the smooth, softly rounded surfaces, the bulges and hollows beneath the palms of my hands and the tips of my fingers. How lovely it is to take in all this beautiful snow-white body with my whole hand! It's so firm, cool and strong, I become enraptured. I wonder if the lion can feel my stroking and understand how much I like it? Just think of having things like this to play with! How happy the general must be to own them and be able to play with them all day long! Most of all I'd like to creep up on to the lion's back and ride on it, but I daren't do that because of the general.

'Hurry up, hurry up!' cries Uncle Georg when we're back on the shore again. 'We've quite a way to go still.'

After a while he swings the rudder round and we glide into a narrow sound winding along between two perpendicular cliff-faces. They are so high, they just touch the vault of the sky. The clouds hide behind them, so only a narrow strip of their dazzling white woolly backs looks out. The water is calm and mirror-like. We can see the crumbling cliff-faces continuing both above and deep down below us. It's like floating into a bottomless ravine.

'Look – the Fire Mountain!' cries Bernt, pointing to the cliff-face on the left.

The mountain consists of fine-grained red stone. A few stunted alders and birches cling at the water's edge, but at the top it is quite bare. It has been ravaged by a forest fire, charred trunks with broken-off tops shooting up here and there out of the cracks, and the grass as reddish brown as a fox's fur. When you draw a deep breath, you can still just make out the smell of smoke. Sometimes there's a glimmer behind the blocks of stone, like evil, glowing eyes staring down at us.

At the very top, the mountain ridge is edged by a whole crowd of black monsters that have petrified into distorted positions, suffocated by the fire just as they were trying to escape. Some of them are stretching out charred stumps instead of arms, others turning their scorched faces to the sky to let out furious screams and curses, some are holding out the black, bony spikes over which the flying skin of their wings had been stretched.

Their mutilated bodies give you no sense of horror.

This is where Michael fought his battle with Satan and his henchmen. When you go past the mountain at sunset, the sky flares above like a sea of fire, the mountain surrounded by flames and, inside the fire, infernal spirits dance and bound about like flickering black spots. They try to get higher and higher up and cling to the rosy edges of the clouds. But the heavenly hosts poke them back with their golden lances and they fall wriggling and tumbling over one another down the burning mountain.

On the other side, the cliff-face is even higher. It lies in eternal shadow. The sun has never shone on its grey, speckled surface, which is overgrown here and there with bracken and is always cold and damp. The damp gushes out of the cracks in the stone and falls in heavy drops down the ledges – in places the cliff-face is streaked from top to bottom with dark lines and covered with trembling green slime. The whole mountain seems to be always weeping and grieving over something.

The dark spruces on the mountain ridge are gloomy and stern.

Although I have never stood on the top, because it's dangerous and actually quite impossible to climb up that dizzy precipice, I know that the Echo lives there. The Echo imitates your voice and repeats everything you say just to annoy you.

I feel ill at ease and avoid talking loudly here in the immediate proximity of the Echo. The protruding rocks hovering above our heads make you feel dizzy and heavy of heart. All the time I can feel the Echo up there observing us, although it is invisible. Supposing it nudged at the mountain so that one of those rocks loosened and hurtled down into the lake just as the boat was passing? Sometimes the whole of the cliff-face seems to be about to tip over on to us like a screen.

We have arrived at the narrowest part of the sound and are heading towards some boulders that rise out of the water. The current is strong and there are crafty underwater stones here that keep themselves well concealed. When you think you are just going to hit one, nothing happens, but when you give the dangerous place a wide berth, you row right on to it.

'Back!' cries Uncle Georg. 'We're going right on to the stone. Right! Right!'

'Ight!' repeats the Echo. The voice is amazingly abrupt and scolding, as if a dog were disguising itself and trying to speak in a human voice.

Mamma presses her lips together and pulls heavily on the left oar, which slips and sends a shower of water all over Grandmother and Uncle Georg.

'Easy now!' snorts Uncle Georg. 'More to the right, I told you!'

The boat swings out away from the stones. Black shadows sweep ahead under the rippling surface, little silver whirlpools gurgling and rippling all round us.

'But that's just where the stone is!' says Grandmother. 'I think you're mistaken, Georg. More to the left.'

'Calm down, Muscha dear!' says Uncle Georg, twisting the rudder to the right with all his might so that the water swirls round the stern. 'I know every stone in this lake. And now, thank goodness, we're out of the shallows!'

'Allows!' snarls the Echo.

At that moment we hear an ominous crash, the boat strikes something underwater and we all fall off our seats. Mamma drops the oar in the water and Bernt, who has hit his knee against the bottom of the boat, starts whimpering.

'Just keep calm!' roars Uncle Georg, standing in the stern. 'The oar, Anni! The oar!'

There is general confusion. The snarling laughter of the Echo rolls maliciously through the sound. The boat wobbles and lurches as if intending to tip the whole lot of us out. The oar appears from somewhere or other and pours a stream of cold water over me.

'Georg dear!' says Grandmother. 'My parasol!'

Then we all see Grandmother's parasol majestically sailing away past the boat, turning round like a wheel in the current, swinging up on the crests of the waves, diving down and shooting up again until it suddenly disappears.

'Zum Kuckkuck!' growls Uncle Georg with annoyance.

'Kuckoo!' sighs the Echo far away.

'You see now, Anni,' mutters Uncle Georg, sitting down at the rudder again, 'if you'd done what I said. . . .'

Mamma defends herself and maintains she had done exactly what Uncle Georg had ordered. Uncle Georg growls and grumbles. But Grandmother says nothing. She takes out her umbrella from under the stern seat and puts it up. As long as Grandmother had her red parasol, the boat looked like a festively decorated ship with resplendent red sails. Now it is like a craft with the message of grief and death on board.

I'm cross with that horrid stone that frightened us all and stole Grandmother's lovely parasol. However much I looked down into the dark waters, I couldn't see him. He must be as big and flat as a giant crab and have a row of shining teeth. Now he's sitting on the bed of the lake with the red parasol over his head, letting goldfish and salamanders admire him.

The shores become less steep and are covered with lush greenery. An unusual clear light lies just above the silent water, which reflects the shady trees of the park, the silver willows and the tangle of rushes dipping their branches into the lake. A thin layer of pollen covers the surface of the water and makes a glistening golden border to our wash, and here and there a fish sparkles like a silver spoon, leaving behind a fine cobweb-like circle in the place where it vanished.

'We'll soon be there,' says Grandmother, closing her umbrella. 'Get ready, children.'

Slowly the bath-house, the jetty and the long road bridge with its striped ribbon of black supports glide towards us. The shady trees of the park are humming with birds and their metallic twittering sounds far across the water. Above all this flickering greenery in various shades Salmela's pointed gable rises against the soft violet arch of the sky, where the clouds lazily creep around like great white cotton-wool hares. Slowly the enchanted palace rises out of the greenery, the tall needle-like spire, the pointed gables, the fiery red roof, the white walls radiating a dazzling light that competes in glory with the clouds.

We're approaching the Holy Grail.

15

JUST AS TEERILÄ IS RULED BY FEMALE TRINITIES, THE AUNTS at Salmela are also three.

Aunt Louise is the smallest – she hardly comes up to Mamma's shoulders – and is the eldest, wisest and most powerful, so is indubitably highest in ranking order. I'm also most afraid of her and never feel really comfortable in her presence. She's the one who shrieks the most and the loudest, her whole crumpled little face trembling and shaking as she lets out her welcoming screech.

'Hullo, hullo! Hullo, dear Anni! Muscha dear! What a lovely surprise!'

Although what she says isn't at all dangerous, I think she is angry and is scolding us. She holds her head slightly back and, as she speaks, she twists her body sideways with little abrupt jerks. Sometimes, when her shriek is particularly angry and shrill, she takes a little hop – just like a cockatoo when it hops on its perch.

Aunt Louise is always dressed in black silk that curves shimmering over her round bosom, on which sits a handsome gold brooch. Her little black eyes dart hither and thither, the irises blurred and as if mouldy round the edges. Her movements are swift and impatient, as if she were always in a fearful hurry, and she rushes ahead of us all through the rooms, flinging the salon doors wide open, talking all the time in her shrill voice so that no one can get a word in edgeways.

Aunt Louise has a cockatoo. As soon as we have gone in and been welcomed, his shrill, angry scream echoes right through the house. When it comes to resources of voice and the ability to make loud noises, he surpasses his mistress in every respect. The more Aunt Louise talks and the longer the welcoming ceremony drags on, the angrier the cockatoo becomes. Aunt Louise's voice gradually fades away and in the end we can't really hear what she is saying, although she is shrieking and gesticulating as hard as she can. The cockatoo clearly can't bear Aunt Louise paying attention to or preferring anyone but him. I can't understand what he's shrieking because he uses cockatoo language. 'Kija, kija. Ka kija!' he screams. He's obviously heaping abuse and curses on us.

When we go into the salon, I stuff my fingers into my ears and can't help blinking all the time. The others screw up their faces in dismay, too, trying to make themselves heard.

In the end, Aunt Louise rushes over to the cage, where the cockatoo is angrily flapping and banging on the bars so that little bits of white down fly out into the room.

'Popotjka!' says Aunt Louise, her voice quite changed, now sugary sweet as she smiles devotedly with her black, toothless mouth, clucks with her tongue and pushes out her lips as if throwing a kiss to the cockatoo. 'Popotjka! Oh, my Popotjka!'

But the cockatoo is furious. He shakes his shimmering white plumage as if he had the ague, fluffs up the tuft of feathers on his head so that the lemon-yellow feathers stand straight up like on a Red Indian, and he heaps another shower of abuse on Aunt Louise. When Aunt Louise approaches the cage, he hops against the bars, curls his crooked black claws and his beak round them and shakes them furiously, then tries to stick his head out to bite Aunt Louise's hand.

It takes quite a while before Aunt Louise manages to make him see reason. Her voice grows softer and more caressing and her toothless mouth floats out into a wider and wider smile. Popotjka's angry screams do grow weaker and less convincing, but he defiantly refuses to change his cockatoo language to Russian, which is what he usually speaks. He pretends he doesn't understand Aunt Louise's outpourings, and now and again clucks mockingly with his tongue, imitating her.

In the end Aunt Louise takes a peanut out of her skirt pocket and sticks it in between the bars of the cage. The cockatoo snatches it and hops up on the swinging ring in the middle of the cage. But he doesn't eat the nut, just puts it on a little metal shelf near his water cup, saving it for another time.

Not until then does he lower his crown of feathers so that they lie flat and obedient along the top of his head in a touching little crest, like a schoolboy who has just flattened his hair with water. He struts about like a cat, stretches his neck and turns his head from side to side as if he could feel Aunt Louise's fingers stroking him fondly down his back. He then responds to Aunt Louise's soft mumblings by repeating the same word several times, quite clearly and in a human voice: 'Popotjka durak! Popotjka durak! Popotjka is a silly.'

'Thank goodness, he's calmed down!' sighs Aunt Louise. 'Forgive me, forgive me, my dear guests! Come in, come in!'

She rushes ahead of us and flings the veranda doors

wide open. We go out on to the veranda, where tea is laid.

Aunt Malla takes second place when it comes to power and dignity at Salmela. She comes in from the garden with a watering-can in her hand and a huge pale-yellow straw hat on her head, so her face is quite hidden. I like Aunt Malla best of all the Salmela aunts. When she has taken off her hat, you can see her shiny pink oval rabbit face and its little slanting eyes sleepily and benevolently peering at you. She is wearing a fine-checked grey blouse and a pleated skirt that looks like crêpe paper. Her hair is whiter than Aunt Louise's and covers her head in fine, wavy humps. She talks slowly and thoughtfully, her hands always folded in her lap.

The most amazing thing about Aunt Malla is that she is always nodding, whether she's talking or sitting there saying nothing, just as if she wished to stress she was in agreement with the entire world as well as herself. Sometimes, when her nodding gets too energetic, I'm frightened her head will come off like the head of a Chinese porcelain doll.

Aunt Gulla is the biggest of the aunts. She looks like a pile of huge black silk cushions stacked on top of each other, everything about her swelling round curves. Her face is large and five-sided, her bushy eyebrows always up on her forehead in a puzzled and distressed expression. She reclines in an armchair on the veranda and you never see her move, except from one armchair to another. Although Aunt Gulla has the softest and kindest voice of all the aunts, and she pats me on the head and puts a toffee in my hand when I shake hers, I like her least of all. She has the lowest place in the ranking order and so you don't have to take any notice of what she says or does.

'My dear guests,' shrieks Aunt Louise, throwing out her hands towards the table and the glistening samovar. 'Sit yourselves down, sit yourselves down and let's have some tea!'

Aunt Malla nods and Aunt Gulla slowly gets up out of her armchair, then sinks sighing down on to a couch beside the tea-table.

But we've hardly sat down at the table before that shindy in the salon starts up all over again. The cockatoo screeches and Aunt Louise's hands shake so that the tea spills into the saucer as she holds the cup under the samovar. 'Poor Popotjka! How nervous he is today,' she says to Grandmother, putting her cup aside. 'Excuse me. . . .'

She rushes into the salon and a moment or two later comes back with the cage in her arms and puts it down beside her on the bench. But there, too, Popotjka is extremely tiresome company, constantly drawing attention to himself and interrupting the conversation with his terrible screeching. Aunt Louise has to bribe him all the time with lumps of sugar and peanuts. Her movements when she serves the tea become more and more impatient and jerky. I'm always afraid there'll be an accident and the cups and plates will start flying out of her hand or she'll pull down the entire table-cloth.

At last Aunt Louise gets cross. She seizes the cage with the flapping cockatoo and rushes off. Then she throws a large bath-towel over the cage. For a few moments Popotjka screeches and rages on worse than ever. You can see the towel moving up and down in little waves at his furious objections to this outrageous punishment. But then it turns deathly silent. The bath-towel is quite still, the grown-ups can talk to each other, and this lasts as long as the cage is covered over.

I wonder what Popotjka is up to inside there. Is he asleep, as he's so quiet? When I've finished my glass of milk and eaten the piece of cake Aunt Louise has put on my plate, I can't resist going over to the cage. I cautiously lift the towel and look inside. The cockatoo's black eye glints angrily and like lightning he at once sinks his black, clawlike beak into the finger I've poked through the bars. Screaming, I rush back to the tea-table.

'Mamma, Mamma!' I shriek. 'The cockatoo bit me. He bit my finger!'

The injury is bleeding impressively and Aunt Malla and Mamma have to bandage it up. As I look at the spots of blood on my trousers and sandals, full of sorrow and self-pity, Popotjka shrieks and yells over in his cage so that it echoes all over the house.

Popotjka must be a very nasty creature. I can't understand why Aunt Louise likes him and always talks to him in such a babbling, honeyed voice.

If the aunts' house gives an impression of being an enchanted castle at a distance, its interior does not correspond at all to your expectations and fantasies. It has rows of high shadowy rooms you're always getting lost in and the shining parquet floors are as slippery as icy streets. Generals in splendid uniforms stare fiercely down from the walls at you, frowning heavily, and here and there is an Empire mirror that breaks the perspective and makes you think there's a whole suite of rooms on the other side of the glass. But when you get closer, you can see your own reflection timidly appearing out of the dimness.

The rooms are full of the most amazing objects: dwarf palm trees, myrtle-bushes and other unknown plants spreading out their dark, leathery leaves in all directions. It's like finding yourself in a primeval forest. Crystal chandeliers glitter from the ceilings and conjure up wonderful rainbow-shimmering spots of sun in the evening light. Silently, they slip across the walls and settle anywhere, on the arm of a chair, on a leaf, on the hem of Grandmother's or Aunt Louise's skirt. I can catch these disembodied colour-creatures in my hand and see my fingers glow red, green and indigo. But when I try to take the mysterious colours with me, the dazzling spot leaps like lightning out of my hand and lands far away on the ledge of the tiled stove or on another piece of furniture.

Glimmering mother-of-pearl shells sit in front of the tiled stove, on the tables and on the stove shelf, some of them spotted like leopards, others rather like delicate pink, glowing fans. Some are as big as dishes, and I squat down on the floor and play boats with them, sailing my brown teddy bear in them round the parquet floor.

After a while, Aunt Malla takes out her collection of shells from the Black Sea and lets me spread them out on the floor. They are all shapes and colours, and I like the kind of small, plum-shaped shells with touching, snoutlike noses best of all. Aunt Malla shows me how to hold the big shells against my ear and listen. I can hear a great roaring, as if from a waterfall, but the voice of the little shells is so tiny you can't make it out, not even if you press them right up against your ear.

But there are other things which are even more bewildering. For instance, the aunts have the head of an elk above the hall door. It looks at you with weary eyes, its thick upper lip scornfully drawn down, its nostrils flaring. Its grey goatee beard twists a long way down below its chin and the terrible spiky antlers splay out like branches of an oak tree. When the salon door suddenly slams behind me and the hall is in semi-darkness, the eyes in the head of the elk slowly start glittering and moving, and follow me, the elk's lips curling into a really sinister smile.

Then there are snow-white owls perched on cupboards and shelves. You *know* they're dead and can't fly off their look-out posts, and yet they frighten you as you creep by, because they sit there so silently, their eyes cold and accusing, and never leaving you.

Aunt Malla's room is just like an orangery, flooded with light and smelling of damp and flowers. The whole room is full of pots, for Aunt Malla grows cacti. Some cacti look like curled-up hedgehogs, angrily splaying out their sharp prickles. Others have cylindrical, articulated trunks and struggle up towards the ceiling, higher and higher every year. Aunt Malla disappears completely behind a palisade of green pillars, as if into a Mexican cactus jungle.

Some of the cacti are in flower, and Aunt Malla points proudly at the lush, scarlet blooms arching gently out of the stems. Only in my dreams have I ever seen such dazzling big flowers before. When I put my face close to them, I can see right into their fiery red blooms, their beauty dangerous, charged with some mysterious force. I can see shimmering little pearls of clear liquid right down inside them, the wreath of stamens, and then the long, thin pistil stretching out like a hungry tongue. Aunt Malla tells me that a flower like that comes out so quickly you can see the petals unfolding with your naked eye, just like a butterfly's wings as it creeps out of the pupa. And all the time she mysteriously keeps nodding.

Behind the palisades of cacti Aunt Malla has a squirrel which wildly leaps about in a cage with several rooms. He entertains us enormously with his tricks. At one end of the cage is a wire cylinder and now and again the squirrel slinks into it, curls up and sets the cylinder whizzing round – as if riding on a merry-go-round. I can't help laughing loudly every time he does this star turn.

Despite my declarations of love, the squirrel is timid. When I stick my fingers in through the bars, he sniffs cautiously at my fingertips so that it tickles and I have to laugh, but then he leaps away in terror and retreats to the back end of the cage.

When Aunt Malla has shown us everything and gone back to the other grown-ups on the veranda, Bernt and I creep carefully back to her room. Although Aunt Malla has expressly forbidden it, we open the cage door to be able to get at the squirrel better and feel him with our hands. But the squirrel doesn't respond at all to our feelings of friendship. Swift as an arrow, he flies out and leaps from Bernt's shoulder up on the curtain, where he squats down, chattering with delight.

A real circus performance then starts, and we nearly

die laughing. The squirrel nips away so quickly, we can hardly keep track of where he is, as he seems to be in all four corners of the room at once. But when he jumps in among Aunt Malla's cacti and knocks over a few pots, it's no longer funny. Bernt whispers that we should creep out and close the door – the squirrel will get tired of his silly tricks and go back into the open cage. But when I see the naughty squirrel continuing his destructive activities, I'm frightened. He breaks off one cactus plant after another and sends the pots crashing down to the floor. When I think how much Aunt Malla loves her cacti, I start screaming my head off. The aunts rush in from the veranda and there's a terrible commotion. I'm sure the squirrel was the only one to enjoy it.

Armed with brooms and butterfly-nets, the aunts chase the squirrel from room to room; curtains are torn down, glass vases tipped over and finally the dreaded Kuno Grim is called in to take us to task. He waves his bamboo walking-stick at us and pinches our ears so hard they smart for a long time afterwards. As soon as I am alone with Bernt again, he hits me because I hadn't stayed still and done what he'd told me.

When I go back to the veranda, red in the face and tearful, a tall, slight boy is standing beside Aunt Gulla's rocking-chair. 'This is Oliver,' says Aunt Gulla. 'Isn't my little man a really big boy?'

I look at Oliver, who smiles at me, and I quickly wipe away a tear.

'Go out and play together now,' Aunt Gulla goes on, putting my hand in Oliver's. 'Show him round, Oliver, and don't let him get up to any more mischief.'

Oliver smiles again at me, and I am at once immensely pleased. Everything is fun and exciting again. 'Come on,' he says.

We walk through a number of rooms out into the kitchen, and from there into the backyard. On the kitchen steps we trip over the dogs lying sunning themselves. They must be as old as Aunt Louise herself, but in contrast to her they have all kinds of ailments that arouse compassion and terror. Some of them are lame, others apparently moth-eaten and have horrid sores on their sides, or they've lost all their teeth. Some are deaf, but all of them are blind, so they can't see us when we come. Their faces are so overgrown with hair, they look like skeins of wool and I can't even see their eyes.

As they drag on their joyless lives there in the twilight of the back steps, they remind me of a crowd of beggars. They sleep all day and don't even bother to chase off the flies buzzing round them, trying to get inside their ears and noses. Now and again one of them wags his tail, as if he could hear his mistress calling him in his dream. Another slowly raises his head and gazes searchingly into the impenetrable darkness, his back and paws trembling, then his head again lowers, weary and abandoned, and his nose sinks down to his forepaws. Everything is as before.

I am reminded of the rich man and Lazarus and say to Oliver that Aunt Louise isn't really kind to her dogs. But he just jokes about Aunt Louise's sentimentality and says she's silly not getting rid of those mummies, which have long since outlived their lives.

A crane is solemnly pacing back and forth in the backyard, now and again picking something up, stretching out her lovely long neck and looking mysteriously at me with her round eye. Her plumage is a wonderful slate-grey colour, her tail feathers elegantly curled as if she had just come from the hairdresser's, her long legs, as thin as wire, moving slowly and ceremoniously, and every time she lifts her leg, she draws in her claws and crooks her foot as condescendingly and with the same dignity as when big Aunt Lala holds out her hand to a gentleman for him to press his lips to it.

To my indescribable joy, the crane slowly approaches and speaks to me. I don't really catch what she is saying, but anyhow she is quite different from all the other cranes, and she speaks in a human voice, using the most courteous and elevated phrases.

All through our conversation I keep hold of Oliver's hand. The crane is much taller than I am, and I have to look up all the time to be able to make out her face. I feel infinitely proud and flattered by her words.

Then the crane sings a song to me and I try to learn it off by heart. It's all about a crane and a heron who loved each other but never succeeded in marrying owing to a series of unfortunate misunderstandings. When the heron proposed, the crane refused him, and when the crane changed her mind and in her turn proposed, the heron turned her down.

All the way home I thought about this peculiar love story going on and on without ever coming to an end, although the solution was within reach all the time. Late that night, when I'm in bed and just falling asleep, I repeat it verse by verse to myself, seeing the crane and the heron in front of me, wading round the marsh and pursuing each other with declarations of love.

16

THE GARDEN BEGINS BELOW THE GRUND AUNTS' VERANDA, stretching a long way along the shore, and is so big you can get lost in it, the narrow, raked, sandy paths twisting and turning through the hedges of roses. They have all kinds of roses, great big cream-coloured ones, clear yellow ones, then red roses of every shade from pale pink to bright satiny red, and dark carmine ones that turn quite black at dusk. Some of them are buds just beginning to come out and as firm as Easter eggs, their petals rolled into cornets and only just curling at the edges. Others are right out and full to the brim with sweet-scented petals.

But mostly they are briar roses with a simple flower of pink petals and a golden button of a stamen in the centre. If you touch a flower, the petals drop off and the paths under the hedges are strewn with little pink petals, glistening in the cobwebs, sticking to the grass stalks, the stone walls and the bushes, and now and again fluttering by like moths.

But the aunts' garden hasn't got only roses in it. It seems as if all the flowers in the world had assembled between the rose-bushes. When you walk along the paths, you find one amazing flower-bed after another full of gigantic sunflowers, as tall as palm trees, a black disc in the middle surrounded by brilliant yellow rays, tall bushes of bluish-purple monkshood, with a little cart drawn by two doves inside the flowers, clumps of foxgloves whose flowers you can thread on your finger like a thimble, and scarlet and orange snapdragons that look like heads of cockerels and can bite your finger, though very slowly, so you hardly feel it. There are pansies there, too, with grave faces, and mignonettes, peonies and delphiniums, little pink daisies like meringues with a yellow, creamy pearl in the middle, and innumerable other flowers whose names I don't know. But when you walk in the rose garden, you get utterly confused by the blaze of colour. At a distance, the flower-beds look like brilliant cloths spread out on the lawn and you see winged dragons, curled-up snakes and shimmering rainbow angel wings, banners and flags.

This rose garden really belongs to Laurin, the King of the Dwarfs, the garden Vittig and Didrik von Bern once upon a time wrecked and cut down with their swords. Here and there you can still see petrified grey dwarfs with their noses cut off, grimly peering out of the dimness of the hedges along the paths. The King of the Dwarfs himself has fallen over and is lying face down in the grass with his amputated feet behind an arbour, slugs and snails crawling all round his neck and his body covered with green patches of lichen as if he had a rash.

Later on, Klingsor conjured the garden up again and filled it with glorious women who danced in gossamer veils below the aunts' veranda. At that time, the Knights of the Holy Grail lived in the house and the girls tried to lure them down into the garden in order to sin. That was where Amphortus got his terrible sores that refused to heal, and the Holy Grail wasn't saved until Parsifal stepped down into the garden and thrust Amphortus' spear right through Klingsor.

Klingsor's realm has been crushed, but after it has rained the garden seethes with all sizes of warty toads clumsily hopping about on the paths. In the evenings at dusk, when the mist sweeps into the garden, you can occasionally see Klingsor's gigantic shadow gliding by, menacingly rising and fumbling with his hands among the tree-tops. A mysterious light creeps out from the mist, shining like a glow-worm, disappearing and appearing again. Bernt says it's only Kuno Grim walking round with a torch in his hand.

'Wait a little while!' says Aunt Malla, leading us over to a green bench. 'The girls will soon be here.'

Neither Bernt nor I had ever played with a girl. When Aunt Malla's benevolently nodding head had vanished behind the roses, I felt almost the same peculiar excitement inside me as on Christmas Eve when the Christmas Goat comes in. We didn't feel like talking to each other. Bernt walked to and fro with his hands behind his back, kicking a little red-and-white speckled stone in front of him. I sat on the bench and slowly drew my finger along a crack in the wood.

Katinka and Nina were second cousins of ours. Grandmother and Mamma had talked about them so often, we were already old acquaintances. I knew that Katinka was seven and so only a little younger than Bernt, and that Nina was my age. But we had never yet met them. Their parents, Uncle Bori and Aunt Paula, were sitting over in the arbour talking to Mamma and Aunt Louise

Aunt Louise. We knew them as well from the stories Grandmother and Mamma had told us.

Uncle Bori has muscles like little apples under his skin because as a child he never left his spinach on his plate and always loved eating the skin on his hot milk. Aunt Paula can climb trees and once lived a whole summer up in an oak tree in which she had built herself a house.

But when we shook hands with Uncle Bori recently, he wasn't at all like any of the other uncles I'd seen before. He had a narrow face pressed together at the sides and running down into a short, straight neck. He had a little, brushlike moustache and wore pince-nez. To me he looked mostly like a mole. His ability to break horseshoes, heave cannons out of ditches and maybe lift whole houses didn't show at all on the outside. Aunt Paula was considerably taller than Uncle Bori. Her thick black hair looked like horsehair and arched like a cupola over her forehead. Her eyes were small and peering, as if she'd got soap in them. It's hard to see how she managed to climb about in trees in her narrow skirt and why her piled-up hair didn't get caught in the branches.

Suddenly a shadow fell across my knees and, when I looked up, Katinka was standing there in a yellow dress, her hair in long, dark plaits. She shook hands and bobbed a curtsy, gold glinting in her mouth when she smiled, and she had some kind of wire brace round her teeth. Bernt at once started talking to her, but I was a little afraid of that wire thing and turned away after greeting her.

'Where's Nina?' said Bernt after a while.

'She said she was shy,' said Katinka. 'I think she's hiding somewhere around here, listening.'

At that moment there was a rustle in the rose-bush behind where Aunt Malla had disappeared, and Nina leapt out on to the path. She was neat and as pretty as a doll, and I at once liked her. Her loose fair hair fell glossily over her shoulders, and in her hands she had a big red rubber ball she was bouncing up and down and catching. Her short blue dress swirled round her so that you could see her little pink trousers, and she had on white shoes and short red-and-blue striped socks.

I wanted to shake hands with her, but she went on leaping about in front of me like Aunt Malla's squirrel, her eyes sparkling, teasingly and inquisitively as if challenging me to come and dance with her as quickly as possible.

'Nina,' called Aunt Paula from the arbour in her singsong voice. 'Don't be so wild. You can't come bathing with us if you keep fooling about like that.'

After a while we all walked through the garden down to the lake. Aunt Louise and Aunt Malla had put up their parasols. Aunt Paula held Mamma's arm and Uncle Bori walked beside them poking his walking-stick into the sand. Every now and again the aunts stopped, Aunt Malla bent down to push aside some stem or branch, and Aunt Louise waved her parasol to draw the others' attention to some particularly lovely flower.

We ran ahead of the others. I did my best to keep close to Nina, but she seemed to have forgotten me and spent all her time talking and laughing with Katinka. The shadows from the leaves trembled like a net over her hair and her brown shoulders and, as she rushed down through the leafy tunnel, she looked like a butterfly, a Common Blue, fluttering ahead of me. She plunged into the shadows, glinting for a moment, then dissolving into a whirl of gold, pale-blue and brownish purplish patches. When she turned round, her hair was standing on end in a mane round her face and her little white shoes flashed so rapidly you hardly had time to see what they were. She was gasping for breath, adjusting her hair-ribbon across her forehead and then, laughing, she clung firmly on to Katinka's arm. 'Today's fun!' she cried, tossing her head back so that her hair fell over her shoulders.

I made an effort to laugh with her, but I wasn't having nearly so much fun as Nina because I desperately needed to pee. I ought to have gone before we even went into the

Grund aunts' house, or at least while we were waiting by the bench for the girls. But Aunt Paula and Uncle Bori had been there all the time, and I was also afraid that meanwhile the girls would come and ask where I was. I was suddenly in so much of a hurry, I had to take a couple of leaps, then stop and press my thighs together until the worst was over. If only I could have hidden behind some bush or other, but the aunts and Uncle Bori behind us would probably have noticed and the girls would have asked why I had run off. Perhaps I could hold on until we got to the bath-house, where you could pee in the water, although we weren't really allowed to.

'Shall we play hide-and-seek?' cried Katinka.

Nina clapped her hands and skipped about on her toes.

At that moment I again had to take a few peculiar leaps and stop as if turned to stone – fortunately in front of a clump of handsome peonies I pretended to look at. I turned my back on the others, grabbed the front of my trousers and bent double over the flowers.

'What are you doing?' said Katinka from behind me.

'I'm smelling the flowers,' I said, without looking up. 'They smell so lovely.'

Katinka lowered her head so that her long, dark plait tickled my cheek. 'I can't smell anything,' she said. 'Peonies don't have any scent.'

Thank goodness it was over again, though a little had come in my trousers. I could feel the moist warmth, and a small dark patch could be seen on the outside, but the girls had probably not noticed anything.

'Oh, you are boring,' exclaimed Nina. 'Only grown-ups smell flowers. Why don't you want to play with us?'

'But I do,' I said, trying to laugh.

Katinka rushed away and Bernt hurried after her. She tried to turn down a side-path, but Bernt caught her. They wrestled and laughed, then both fell over on the lawn.

Nina pouted and gave me a disappointed, mocking look. 'Can't catch me!' she cried, and I rushed after her through the leafy tunnel.

Patches of sunlight and shadow whirled past, the branches dancing, and sometimes everything was as striped as a mattress and winking like sunlight through lattice-work. A branch slapped me across the face. But Nina's blue dress was already fluttering far away in the sunlight where the path opened out into a gateway. One moment Nina was hovering in the air, swinging round, then she disappeared like a bird as it lands on the ground.

Then everything became unbearable again. I ran on, not knowing where I was. Nina's blue dress winked in the hedges into which she had crept, but I rushed past as if I hadn't even seen her. Quickly, quickly – so that no one could find me. I was saved.

I turned down a side-path and caught a glimpse of the nasty grinning face of a dwarf. I couldn't go there, for that was where the aunts and Uncle Bori were walking with Mamma. She waved at me and the aunts called out to me to turn back, because the bath-house was in a completely different direction. But I ran on.

Thorns pricked me as I crawled through a briar hedge, scratching my forehead, elbows and thighs, cobwebs fastened on to my face and a wasp buzzed menacingly round my head.

When I had at last got through the hedge, Kuno Grim was there, walking to and fro on the path, smoking. He wagged his finger at me. Horrified, I took away the hand that had been clutching at my trousers and rushed on.

Now, at last, I could. I was just by the stone wall round the rose garden. No one could see me there. It was still and quiet, nothing but flies buzzing sleepily round the flowers. As if in a dream, I pulled up my blouse and at first I couldn't get the buttons undone and one of them came off.

But I'd hardly let my trousers down and watched the glittering stream spurt over the briars and the wall when an angry screech made me double up and pee spurted all over my hands and the trousers round my ankles. When I looked up, a gigantic bird with a crown on its head and with golden yellow and azure breast feathers was sitting on the wall. He flapped his wings menacingly and stretched out his neck. Then he let out another of his penetrating screeches so that everyone would notice what I was doing, looking at me with his round eye and bobbing his head a few times as if pecking at me, then contemptuously turned his back on me, his rainbow-coloured tail sweeping over the stone wall.

I didn't dare pee, so I fled, my trousers hindering my movements, so I tripped, fell headlong into the grass among the rose petals and scrambled up again, the shrill, accusing screech echoing behind me all the time, reverberating all over the garden.

I was now behind the arbour where the crippled King of the Dwarfs lay flat on his face in the grass. I got ready to pee, but only a few drops would come.

At that moment I heard running footsteps and a rustle in the hedge behind me. I quickly managed to pull up my trousers and button them. They looked awful, the whole of the front of one trouser-leg dark and glistening.

'Oh, there you are!' cried Nina. She pushed the branches aside and appeared out of the hedge. 'What are you doing? You weren't supposed to be hiding! You're supposed to be catching me!' She took me by the hand. 'Come on, we must hurry. The others will soon be at the bath-house.'

It was fun holding Nina's hand and running beside her. Sometimes our shoulders banged against each other and her hair swept over my face. I tried to show her how fast I could run, but Nina followed as if floating alongside me. We couldn't find our way out of the labyrinth of hedges and paths.

'I called out to you as you ran past,' Nina gasped. 'But you didn't hear me.'

She turned her happy, excited face towards me. But at that very same moment her look changed, her eyes turned huge and round, then dark and solemn. She said nothing, but looked me up and down in some surprise.

Then she turned her head away. I knew at once she had seen and understood everything.

'Come on!' she cried, without looking at me. 'I know the way now. There's the bed of fritillaries.'

She ran on again and I followed, but now she was no longer holding my hand.

17

AUNT LOUISE AND AUNT MALLA WERE SITTING ON A BENCH outside the bath-house talking to Uncle Bori, but the others were inside the hut. Aunt Paula let us in when we knocked on the door.

'Oh, how sweaty you are. Remember now, you mustn't go into the water until I say so.'

It was dim and cramped inside the hut. I quickly took off my blouse and sandals, my undershirt and the horrible trousers. No one had noticed anything.

'Boys and girls should get used to seeing each other naked,' Mamma said as she sat on the bench unbuckling her shoes. 'Then they have a natural approach to each other from the start.'

'Of course,' said Aunt Paula, turning round to hang up her jacket. 'It can't do them any harm when they're still so young.'

It was so bright outside, I had to look down and screw up my eyes when I opened the door. The lake was there waiting for us with its soft, lapping waves, its cool freshness, its smell of rushes and the dancing glitter of the sun prickling your eyes.

I was transformed in some mysterious way. I was just as white and weightless as the light around me, and I looked down with surprise at my naked body, which had suddenly acquired a strange sensitivity that both delighted and embarrassed me. I could feel the hot boards under my feet, the wind playfully flowing round me and breathing against my chest, the sun burning my shoulders and back. When my hands brushed against my bare skin, someone seemed to be caressing me, so at first I hardly dared move.

I squatted down and looked into the water. The waves suddenly seemed to stand still – I was flying at a tremendous speed on a magic carpet across the lake. I clung on to the jetty as hard as I could because I was afraid of losing my grip and plunging down into the dark depths below. In the end I was so dizzy I had to look up. But then I was on the bath-house jetty again, the pool enclosure sleepily heaving up and down on its floating barrels, creaking and squeaking now and again like a ship at sea. Black snakes were wriggling beneath the buttresses, then sometimes fell apart in great trembling circles.

The girls came out after a while, but they weren't naked as I had expected. Katinka still had her shift on and Nina her pink trousers, so her bare top and chubby shoulders were exposed. Her nipples were even smaller than mine and her stomach stuck out, her tummy button looking at me like an eye. I was very disappointed, because I'd have liked to see what Nina looked like without any clothes on.

'Can your pappa dance on the water?' said Nina. 'Mine can. He lifts his hands above his head and spins round and round like this and sings tra-la la la.'

I felt peculiar standing in front of her naked like that, talking while she stared at that place. But Mamma had said it was good for boys and girls to see each other naked and it was nothing to be ashamed of.

I tried to explain that my pappa could do anything. When he dived into the lake, water spurted up higher than the tree-tops and it started raining all over the lake. And when he was angry, he could make the lake into one great waterfall like the Niagara Falls. Anyone who hadn't managed to get out of the water simply drowned.

'When is he coming?' said Nina, her eyes wide. 'I want to see when he goes swimming with my pappa.'

'I don't know,' I said. 'He's always away in St Petersburg building a railway.'

The door opened and Mamma and Aunt Paula came out. They had put on their striped bathing-costumes and looked like zebras.

'Wait here until we come back,' said Mamma, stepping down into the pool. 'You've not cooled down enough yet.'

Her breasts floated up as she stood in the water and one of them slipped out of her neckline so that she had to stuff it back. Then she threw herself forward with a dull surge and glided after Aunt Paula through the opening into the lake. She scissored with her legs and her striped body looked distorted through the water, shortened like a dwarf's. Aunt Paula's head and hers were soon far away and Mamma raised her hand to wave to us, then both of them disappeared into the liquid gold of the glittering sunlight spreading over the lake.

Nina had squatted down beside Katinka, her arm round her neck, and she was whispering something in her ear. Both of them looked at me and giggled. I could feel myself going red and looked away. Were they laughing at me because I had boasted about my pappa, or had Nina told Katinka about my mishap with my trousers? In that case she was a sneak and I would never speak to or play with her again.

Without saying anything, I left the others and climbed out on to the piles round the pool outside the canvas wall. The barrels bobbed up and down beneath me and burnt my feet when I stepped on them. I had to swallow to stop the tears coming, but I still don't know why I was so miserable. Nothing was fun any longer, and I should have given a lot to be somewhere else and not have to listen to Bernt's and the girls' voices behind me.

Why was I nothing but a little boy everyone could laugh at and tease? Why was I just me and no one else?

Then I heard Nina calling me and, when I turned round, I saw she was out on the piles, too, holding on to the canvas wall. 'Help me!' she cried. 'I daren't go any further.'

Then everything was fun and exciting again. I held out my hand to her and she squeezed it so hard it almost hurt. She squealed when the barrel she stepped on sank under the water and turned round.

After we had got round the corner, it wasn't so dangerous any more, for the platform of boards the grown-ups used to sunbathe on was there. We lay down beside each other, the canvas wall above billowing and crackling in the wind, the sky blue, and a great white cloud like a winged llama slowly glided out from behind the wall, its head gradually loosening from its neck and sailing away. Then it dissolved and fell apart into white fluff like a dandelion head. It was lovely lying there quite still beside Nina, listening to the rippling and clucking of the water below us, as if we were going somewhere far, far away. When you closed your eyes, everything turned a flaring red all around, as if you were lying under a purple curtain.

'Children, come away from there at once!' Mamma's voice was angry and commanding.

Mamma is always so difficult. She keeps thinking some accident will happen to us and she forbids everything that's fun, as if the whole world were full of horrible and dangerous things wanting to do us nothing but harm. She thinks all scissors are waiting to be allowed to poke out our eyes, all rocks are lying in wait to trip us up and break our legs and all branches and boards intend to break the moment we climb up on them. The wind blows only to make us ill, and the water is always waiting to suck us down into its cold, dark depths. She thinks she has to remind us constantly about all those things, so that we'll remember to be careful.

It was especially annoying when Mamma behaved like that in the presence of Aunt Paula and the girls, just as if I were an infant who didn't understand anything and couldn't take care of myself.

'Come on now, do as you're told!' shouted Mamma, the water pouring off her bathing-costume down on to the steps. 'Haven't I told you not to climb on the barrels? And now egging Nina on to be disobedient too!'

'Can't I stay here, Mamma?' whined Nina.

'No. Come here!' said Aunt Paula. 'Aunt Anni is quite right.' But then she turned to Mamma and I heard her say: 'I don't think it's really all that dangerous. Children can take care of themselves as long as you give them a little freedom.'

It's always like that. Other children's mothers understand that children must be allowed to climb about on the barrels round a pool. But Mamma never understands things like that and makes you ashamed in the presence of other mothers and children.

'Get undressed, girls,' said Aunt Paula, once we were back on the jetty again. 'You can go into the water now.'

She pulled Katinka's shift over her head and then seized the struggling Nina, who pulled down her trousers and leapt out of them with one great bound.

Suddenly the girls were standing quite naked in front of me. I tried to look to see what they really looked like, but it wasn't easy, because they were leaping and prancing about all the time, kicking up their legs and throwing up their arms. Katinka had a funny sway-back and her round bottom stuck out a little at the back, and Nina's hair swirled round her head like a golden mane. She looked just like one of those chubby angels in Grandmother's Bible – the ones that dance on the clouds. And yet there was something that wasn't quite right. I had never seen that soft, gliding movement she used to stick out her stomach and bend at the hip before. And I only caught a tiny glimpse of her willie for a moment, but it was awfully small and must have stuck to the thigh she was flinging up, so I couldn't see what it was like at all.

After a while we went down into the pool and Mamma stood in the hut doorway with a furry white towel in her hands, ready to receive us when we came out.

'Dip down in the water!' she cried. 'One, two, three! You'll only get cold like that.'

I was a little scared at first and shuddered when the cold water rose up my body and seemed to divide me in two. I had to take a deep breath and couldn't breathe out again for a while. But then it was over. It was lovely to feel the water's soft, cool embrace round your body, the waves lapping against your armpits and the palms of your hands, and carefully lifting you up as if someone wanted to tip you over for fun. 'Look!' I cried to Nina, holding on to the edge so that my legs floated up. It was like being in a hammock, the waves rocking me slowly up and down. But Nina didn't dare come out to me. She sat on the steps, half in the water, splashing with her hands and feet.

Bernt and Katinka were splashing each other. I also started jumping and splashing all round me. Magnificent rainbows flared up over the water, sometimes as if angel wings had fluttered through the sunny vapour and brushed the surface. In the end everything dissolved into a glowing silvery golden glitter, but then I suddenly slipped and fell backwards. Everything round me went dark and glassy green, and I could neither breathe nor shout for help. For a moment I managed to get my face out of the water – everything had turned silvery white, but then I sank back again into the darkness where a ghostly silence reigned.

I don't know how I finally managed to get back on my feet. Suddenly the rippling surface of the water, the canvas walls and Bernt and Katinka were all there again. I was so frightened I couldn't make a sound. Water was running down my face and stinging my nose and throat, so I had to cough and splutter to get my breath back. Only gradually did I notice that I could breathe again.

'I drowned!' I cried to Bernt and Katinka, but they were much too busy playing some game to bother about me.

'Mamma! Aunt Paula!' I cried. 'I drowned! I fell over and lay right under the water.'

'Why are you shouting?' said Mamma, not even bothering to listen and turning back to talk to Aunt Paula again. 'Come on out now and don't make up any more nonsense. You're quite white round your nose.'

I rushed over to the steps where Nina was sitting. 'Did you see?' I shrieked. 'Did you see – I drowned?'

But Nina just kicked water at me and escaped up the steps.

'But it's true, it's true, I drowned!' I exclaimed with annoyance. 'Come over here and I'll tell you about it.'

'Don't be silly,' said Bernt. 'You were under the water for about five seconds. You can't drown in such a short time.'

'You're fibbing!' cried Nina, looking out from behind Aunt Paula's back. 'I'm not coming.' She stuck out her tongue at me.

'Come on out at once!' shouted Mamma. 'Didn't you hear what I said?'

Shivering, I climbed up the steps and let Mamma wrap me in the towel. She swung me to and fro and rubbed me so that my whole body smarted and glowed like fire.

Nina was already dressed when I appeared red and steaming in the semi-darkness of the hut. 'Is it true, what you said?' she asked me.

'What do you think? Of course I drowned, and I'd be quite dead now if I wasn't such a good swimmer. I fell over and swam miles under the water, ending up on the outside of the pool where it's terribly deep – though then I got back through the opening. It was fun down there under the water and I talked to the fish swimming over my head.'

'But why did you fall over?' said Nina.

'Didn't you see the angels flying back and forth? They're usually invisible, but when I splashed water on them, I was sometimes just able to see their wings. I saw the shadow of a black wing that hit out at me – it was the black angel's. My guardian angel was already holding out his hand to me when I fell. . . .'

I could see it all in front of me now, the way I fought with the black angel down in the water, the way he clutched on to me, trying to drag me down to the bottom of the lake, but I had won in the end and wrenched myself free from his grasp. He had looked like a gigantic black crab.

'Feel my muscles!' I said, clenching my fist and lifting my arm. 'Aren't they terribly hard?'

Nina cautiously pinched my arm. Then she looked at me and burst out laughing. 'But you did make all that up, didn't you?'

18

'COME OVER HERE, CHILDREN!' SAID AUNT GULLA, SITTING UP on the couch. 'I've got a little surprise for you. Here!'

She reached out for a bag lying on the table, untied the red ribbon round it, and suddenly four glimmering eggs were lying in her lap. 'There's one egg for each of you,' she said, sharing them out between us.

'Oh, a golden egg!' cried Nina. 'May I look at yours, Riki?'

We showed each other our eggs and compared them. Mine was silver, Bernt's glistening crimson and Katinka's azure blue. The surface was slightly rough and sparkled as if thousands of coloured stars were constantly lighting up and going out inside.

'Where did you get them? Who brought them?' we asked in astonishment at this unusual splendour.

'The Firebird,' sighed Aunt Gulla, leaning back. 'The Firebird brought them.'

'Huh, they're made of chocolate,' said Bernt. 'Aunt Luscha once gave me one like it. You can eat them.'

'Yes of course they're chocolate,' said Aunt Gulla, nodding. 'Why shouldn't the Firebird lay chocolate eggs?'

'You're joking,' said Bernt. 'You buy them in a shop.'

'May we eat them?' said Nina.

'Yes, of course, children dear, you eat them,' puffed Aunt Gulla. 'That's why he laid them last night.'

'Listen!' said Nina, shaking her egg by her ear. 'There's something inside.'

I examined mine and realized that it was the same. When you shook the egg, you could hear and feel something bumping about inside. The discovery made the egg even more wonderful. Nina could hardly control herself.

'What is it? I want to see! How do you open the egg, Aunt Gulla?'

Aunt Gulla's eyebrows rose and she smiled mysteriously.

'Yes, I wonder what it is?'

'I know!' cried Nina. She looked at me and laughed delightedly. 'It's a little chicken. The Firebird's little baby. It's banging with its beak and wants to get out.'

Aunt Gulla showed us how to peel the gleaming silver paper off the eggs. When I bit into my egg, it broke and a whole lot of brown pieces and something small and shiny fell tinkling to the floor. I bent down and picked up a little ring with a blue stone in it.

'A ring! A ring!' cried Nina jubilantly. 'Look, I've got one too!'

We compared rings. Nina's was like mine, a thin, graceful gold hoop with a drop-shaped thick bit, out of which the stone peeped like an eye. But the stone in Nina's ring was red. Katinka had found a pin with forget-me-nots on it, and Bernt had a little gold heart.

'Goodness!' said Nina, smearing chocolate over her chin and cheeks with the back of her hand. 'These rings cost a hundred million marks. They're real gold and real jewels.'

'I think they're fake,' said Bernt. 'You don't put real jewels in chocolate eggs.'

'No, they're real,' insisted Nina. 'Look how my stone sparkles in the light!'

'Good gracious, what do you look like!' cried Aunt Gulla. 'Eat the chocolate up now and come over here so that I can wipe your face.'

When we'd finished, Bernt and Katinka ran down into the garden. But Nina and I stayed with Aunt Gulla and asked her to tell us about the Firebird. She sighed heavily, swept her flowered shawl round her so that it hid her arms and hands, then she started.

'Far far away in the east, where the sun rises, that's where he lives, the Firebird. In the daytime he stays on the mountain-tops and bathes in the sunlight. The air there is as clear as crystal and it is so quiet you can hear the snow melting, the buds opening and the flowers coming out. He grazes there in an emerald-green meadow, pecking up golden acorns. Sometimes he sings to the sun, or plays with his own shadow, or leans over the mirror of the spring under the oaks, his wings outspread. A great many people have tried to capture him, because one single piece of his down is worth more than sacks of gold, and kings have sent their huntsmen to lay snares for him. But they have all come back empty-handed or died in the ravines of the mountain. The Firebird ripped their nets to pieces and flew up to the topmost peaks where no one could follow him.'

'But that's awful for him,' said Nina. 'Why are people so horrid?'

'No, not awful,' said Aunt Gulla, smiling and looking dreamily ahead of her. 'He's happy. It's so wonderfully quiet and peaceful and beautiful there, and anyone allowed to live there should weep with joy. But let me go on. You see, children, he knows that old women like me don't want to capture or kill him, like those greedy kings. He knows we like plants and animals, and that he doesn't have to be afraid of anyone here. So he comes here at night sometimes, to dance in our garden.'

'What does he look like?' I asked. 'Has he got a gold crown on his head and are his breast feathers all blue? Does his tail seem to be full of dancing spots of sunlight?'

'You're probably thinking of the peacock?' said Aunt Gulla, stroking my head. 'No, he's much bigger and more beautiful. And his plumage is a golden red, like the sunrise.'

'I know!' cried Nina. 'He's like a rooster!'

'No, not a rooster. More like a pheasant. But you see, his feathers glow like flames and burn you if you take them in your hand. When it's really dark and the stars are out, he comes swooping across the sky like a burning arrow and sinks down behind the trees over there. Then he dances in among the roses.The whole garden glows as if it were the middle of the day. And Crane and Popotjka and all the little birds stand watching and marvelling over the way he can dance.'

'Ooh, have you seen him?' we whispered. 'Have you seen him dancing?'

'Goodness gracious, what an idea!' said Aunt Gulla, raising her eyebrows and shaking he head. 'He is so shy, he would never come back if he saw me spying on him. Anyhow, he doesn't come until after midnight, and poor old ladies like me can't stay up that late. But one night when I couldn't sleep and got up to take some medicine, I saw the fiery light glimmering among the bushes. Gospodi pomilui, what can that be? I said to myself, rubbing my eyes. For it was flashing and sparkling in among the roses like the most wonderful firework display I've ever seen.'

'Fireworks!' we gasped, looking at each other.

'Yes, just like fireworks,' said Aunt Gulla in a stifled, mysterious voice. 'Fountains of fire spouting forth, flaring feathers and whole clusters of red-and-green stars shooting and crackling up towards the dark clouds, the sky billowing like a curtain and a shower of golden sparks constantly floating down into the garden. Finally I was so giddy, I fell into an armchair, my head whirling from looking up for so long.'

We both laughed with delight at the thought of how beautiful it must have been.

'Well, then, the Firebird isn't arrogant, although he's so proud and lovely. Dear little birds, he calls suddenly in the middle of his wildest pirouettes. How lovely and pretty you are. Come, let us dance and be happy together. And so they dance all night, the Firebird and Crane and Popotjka, the little birds chattering, the grasshoppers singing in the bushes and the roses breathing clouds of scent all over them. He doesn't open his wings and fly away into the glowing eastern light until the Morning Star winks above the tree-tops over there.

'Tjudo tjudo, divo divnoje,' said Aunt Gulla to end her story, for she had told us all this in Russian.

'But how did you get the eggs?' I asked her, twisting the ring where the Firebird's blue stone was flashing. 'Did he have them with him when he came?'

Aunt Gulla lifted her hand dismissively under her shawl and sighed.

'So you want to know everything, do you? When I opened the window this morning, Crane stepped up, bowed and said: Matusjka Aglaja Igorovna, the Firebird was here tonight. He sends his regards and thanks you and wishes you a long life – you and your sisters – for receiving him so well and having the sandy space where he dances in front of the fritillaries raked nice and smooth. Flowers shall bloom, bees gather honey and everything that flies and crawls in the garden shall flourish and praise the Highest. Then he asked me to convey to you that he had laid four chocolate eggs under the bush of yellow roses in the corner. The children may have them if they promise never to do any harm to plants or animals.

'Well, I took my stick and toddled off into the garden. And when I pushed aside the branches of the rose-bush – imagine, there in the grass were the four eggs glittering so brightly, it hurt my eyes. Tjudo tjudnoje! Divo divnoje!'

'Why did Crane say that – the flowers shall bloom?'

'She was just telling me what the Firebird had said. In thanks for being allowed to dance here, he makes it so that everything lasts and becomes more and more beautiful year by year. Look how the roses are blooming over there!'

'I saw him,' I whispered to Nina as soon as we were alone together again. 'I saw the Firebird. Don't you believe me?'

Nina looked doubtfully at me. 'You made that up. I don't believe you.'

'But it's true, really. I saw him here in the garden. He was screeching, up on the wall. Come on, let's go and look for him.'

Nina objected, and said Aunt Gulla had told us the Firebird had flown away at dawn. It was difficult to convince her that Aunt Gulla, who spent most of the day lying on her couch, couldn't know everything about the Firebird, and that he might well be hiding somewhere in the garden in the daytime. I had seen him as large as life, hadn't I, a few days ago, and also knew where his hiding-place was? In the end Nina was also eager to see him, so we ran out into the garden.

'Here!' I whispered, as we stood by the stone wall covered with briar roses, where the brilliant golden bird had frightened me. 'This is where it was. He flapped his wings and scared me so badly, I ran away.'

Nothing had changed, cobwebs and rose petals all

over the ground, and that horrid branch I'd tripped over. It was still, the sun blazing down, flies buzzing sleepily and shadows trembling in a network over Nina's shoulders and face. But there was no sign of the bird. However long we waited for him to show himself up there on the wall, things remained just the same. Finally, I began to doubt I really had seen him. Perhaps I'd just dreamt it, or imagined it all and something quite different had frightened me into running away. When Nina wanted to know how I happened to have met the Firebird, I answered evasively. I didn't want anyone to know how shameful I had been in front of the bird, but naturally that didn't make what I'd said about seeing him any more believable.

'He's not here,' said Nina. 'Come on, let's go and look for him in the place where he danced at night.'

But the sandy patch was also totally empty, and under the bush of yellow roses where the Firebird had laid his eggs there wasn't the slightest bit of down left. We looked for tracks in the sand, but it had been newly raked. Nina did find an impression that looked like a bird's foot, but it couldn't have been the Firebird's because it was too small. It must have been from one of the birds dancing with him. However much we searched, looking behind hedges and calling out to him, he was nowhere to be seen. Aunt Gulla was probably right when she said he had flown off in the morning before the sun had even risen.

We bumped into Crane pecking in the sand behind the kitchen garden. She didn't want to tell us anything about Firebird's visit, but just turned her back on us in annoyance and stalked off on her long legs. Then it started to rain and we had to abandon our attempts to catch up with her.

'She's yearning for Heron,' I explained to Nina as we ran home. 'I suppose she thought Heron would also come last night to dance with her.'

When Nina didn't understand, I again sang the song I had learnt about the Crane.

'Maybe Popotjka knows something,' said Nina when we had gone indoors. 'Let's go and ask him.'

But Popotjka was furious. He was tired after last night's party and had fallen asleep on his perch, his head tucked under his wing so that only the little yellow tuft stuck out. I had to wake him by poking him with a penholder I sneaked from Aunt Louise's desk. He screeched so loudly, we leapt in terror away from the cage and I dropped the penholder on the floor.

'Kija, kija, ka ka kija!' screamed Popotjka, raising his lemon-yellow crest like a fan to frighten us properly.

'Kija, kaja!'

'What's the matter, Popotjka?' called Aunt Louise, rushing in. 'Have you hurt Popotjka?'

'Hurt! Popotjka hurt!' shrieked Popotjka angrily. 'Killa kakilla. Hurt!'

'You should be ashamed of yourselves,' said Aunt Louise. 'Teasing a poor innocent bird! Naughty children! And who gave you permission to take my pen? Shame on you!'

She took both of us by the ear and led us out of the room.

19

IT WAS RAINING AND WE DIDN'T REALLY KNOW WHAT TO DO. I suggested we should play horses and ride on each other's backs, and Bernt wanted us to be elephant hunters and creep into Aunt Malla's room and shoot her, as she was a large, dangerous elephant. But the girls didn't want to.

Then Nina suddenly clapped her hands and started whirling round the room, mincing about and flapping her arms as if flying, then she stretched up, closed her eyes, shuddered from head to toe, and with her head thrown back, pranced on the tips of her toes back across the parquet floor, hopped up to me, bobbed and swirled away so quickly her dress stood out like a wheel. She was singing.

'Dear little Heron
I like thee.
Dear little Heron
Come and marry me.'

'What do you mean?' I exclaimed, drawing a deep breath. 'Why are you singing Crane's song?'

'Crane's song?' Nina stopped and looked at me with wide eyes, then she burst out laughing. 'Can't you see I'm Crane?' she said. 'That's why I'm dancing and singing like this. Look, here's my ring.'

'But I don't want to be Heron,' I said. 'I'm the Firebird.' I jumped up and bounded all round Nina.

'No, don't let's play at being birds,' said Katinka. 'Let's play we're really married like grown-ups. We'll get the dolls and play pappa and mamma. That's much more fun.'

'Yes, that'll be much more fun!' cried Nina with delight. 'We'll get married properly with rings and all, like grown-ups. You can have Bernt and I'll have Riki.'

A little later, Nina and I were standing in front of Katinka. She had wrapped Aunt Louise's black mantilla round her and was reading out of a book in a hollow voice.

'In the Holy of Holies. In the name of the Father, the Son, the Moon and the Holy Hand. I hereby marry you through the Hallelujah of Love and Affection. For ever and ever. Amen. That's that,' she said, closing the book. 'Exchange rings!'

'This isn't a game,' said Nina, threading the ring on my finger. 'You must always think of me when you're at home, and not play with any other girl. Promise me?'

'Yes,' I said, looking down at my ringed hand, Nina's red stone glowing like a dried drop of the Firebird's blood. Our game seemed to have acquired meaning for the first time and was no longer ordinary playing that could come to an end at any time. Now it also entailed something for the future.

'When we're grown up, we'll get married properly and have lots of children.'

'Yes,' I said, and it all seemed very solemn. It was fun standing so close to Nina, feeling the touch of the soft arm she had thrust under mine, and the hair that kept tickling my cheek.

'You're my husband!' She said it in such a matter-of-fact way and looked at me every time so seriously that I felt a peculiar shiver run through me.

Then she suddenly let go my arm, looked teasingly at me and ran over to Katinka. The girls whispered and giggled, looking at us now and again. They stayed there so long, I got tired of it all and felt like going away. But then Katinka came over to me. 'You haven't kissed Nina yet,' she said. 'Married people usually do that.'

I could feel myself going red, but I had no objection to obeying Katinka. I put my face up to Nina's and pressed my lips against her warm, crimson mouth. She responded to the kiss, but then at once wiped her mouth with the back of her hand.

Then it was Nina's turn to kiss me. I expected her to kiss me on the mouth, but she took a little jump and fleetingly brushed her lips against my forehead. With a teasing laugh, she leapt away and started whirling round the room. It was like a little animal nosing at me.

20

EVER SINCE THEN, I AM ALWAYS NINA'S HUSBAND WHEN WE visit Salmela. As soon as we arrive, she's there on the steps and runs towards me to be the first to shake hands. We sit next to each other at table and drink out of similar china mugs with a deer painted on the outside. When we look at the flowers in the rose garden, we hold hands, and when all four of us play ball, Nina always throws me the red rubber ball that spins and bounces so amusingly. We do everything together. Nina is always beside me or so near we can call to each other about what we're thinking or to show each other some amusing thing we've found.

At home, I often think about having a friend and playmate over there beyond the lake in the aunts' enchanted castle, and that I can tell her everything which happens here at home. In that way everything which happens to me is twice as much fun. I can hear myself telling Nina everything, see her astonished, happy face in front of me, and every morning I wait with excitement to hear Mamma say: 'We're going to Salmela today.'

We've found a really good hiding-place by the wall in the rose garden where there are jasmine- and lilac-bushes, and when you crawl in between them, you at once seem to be inside a house with a roof and walls and a smooth floor to sit on. No one can see us. We keep a look-out for anyone walking in the garden, or watch the amazing creatures buzzing in the greenery and crawling on the ground. But we mostly talk about what we'll do when we're grown up. Sometimes Nina goes and fetches her dolls and other toys, and we play mamma and pappa.

She comes with her dress held up over her stomach

and her arms full of dolls, then spreads them carefully out on the ground in front of me.

'Look how many children! Aren't you pleased?'

It's difficult to count them all and distinguish one from the other. I never manage to learn all our children's names. Some of them are big, knobbly boys and girls with rigid, surprised eyes and small, kiss-covered mouths. The girls have curly tufts of hair sticking out of caps sewn on their heads. The boys are bare-headed and their hair is just painted on like a glistening cap on their hard, round heads. Some of the dolls are as small as a little finger, naked and quite stiff, so they can only stand upright or lie on their backs. But they're neater than the others and their very smallness arouses a special feeling of tenderness. Then there's a hairy white bear that has lost one eye. 'He's our child, too,' says Nina. 'For if I want to, I can give birth to animals.'

Last of all, she comes along carefully carrying a big, round-cheeked doll with an alabaster-white complexion and a fringe of thick, black eyelashes along the rim of her lowered eyelids. 'Her name's Irina,' whispers Nina. 'She's not a doll but a real baby. No, you mustn't touch her, just look, because she's alive. Look!'

She sits Irina up and, to my astonishment, Irina opens her eyes and looks round with a condescending, bored look. Then she starts sinking back with a pitifully thin whimper and closes those trembling eyelids. 'Poor little thing!' says Nina, pressing Irina movingly to her breast. 'She's so terribly tired.'

We cook food on Nina's little toy stove. Nina lays the table with her doll's china and then we feed the children. Irina gets the best food and the most toffees. But all she wants to do is to sleep, and she whimpers so pitifully and sadly when Nina picks her up, Nina's eyes fill with tears. The smallest dolls are so small they can't eat cooked food but have to have breast milk. Nina pulls down her dress so that the pale little nipple is exposed and shows me how the doll puts its mouth against it and sucks.

But most of all, I like pretending our cabin is a nest two rock buntings have made. Once, when the girls came to see us, Nina put her finger on the rock bunting and said it was the prettiest of all the birds. Aunt laughed and said that Nina thought that because the rock bunting looked rather like her. And that was probably true. The rock bunting is the smallest of all the birds in the picture. It is golden red and has a round helmet of feathers on its head. In the front, the helmet stretches to the very tip of its beak, so that it looks as if the rock bunting had a human mouth and its big, shiny eye stares just like Nina's.

When we're playing, I'm the cock bunting and Nina is the hen bird. She lays eggs in our hut and I fly around outside, waving my arms and crying 'Kalong! Klong! Klong!' Then I go in and look at the lovely round stones Nina plucks out from under her skirt. Then the stones are exchanged for dolls, which Nina wraps in bits of cloth and the doll's blankets so that nothing can be seen of them. She squats down over them and spreads her skirt out. While she's sitting on the nest, I sit outside on the ground singing to her, or flying around the garden looking for food. I pick briar roses, poppy heads and jasmine flowers, then push them carefully in between Nina's half-open lips. When the eggs hatch out, we both fly round the garden. Sometimes we fly together, but often meet first at the opening to the nest and flap past each other. 'Kalong! Kalong!' twitters Nina. 'Have you got anything for the youngest?'

'Kololoo! Kololaa!' I sing. 'Cocoa fruit and crab-apples.'

21

BUT SUDDENLY EVERYTHING IS DIFFERENT, AND I CAN'T understand why it has all come to an end and Nina is just unkind and keeps teasing me.

It started one afternoon when Mamma decided we were to play Cock-a-Snook. We were playing in Aunt Malla's room, Pappa, Uncle Bori, Dr Montelius and some uncles I didn't know. All the aunts and girls had gone into the hall. Uncle Bori got up and closed the door behind them. Each one of us was to choose someone from those absent and when Uncle Bori asked me whom I wanted, of course I replied 'Nina'.

It was great fun when one aunt after another came in through the door and didn't know who had chosen her, so had to go out again while everyone laughed. Aunt Malla stood in front of me and I cocked a snook at her, and everyone shrieked with laughter and chased her away. Aunt Malla smiled, screwed up her eyes and nodded like a Chinese doll, but then Dr Montelius threw himself back in his armchair howling with laughter and bumped into a flower-pot. All the cacti rocked and swayed like a forest in a storm, and Aunt Malla had to rush over to stop them falling.

Nina dawdled when the door was opened. She opened her eyes wide and, with her finger in her mouth, she looked at all the uncles sitting lined up against the wall. But when our eyes met, she quickly took her finger out of her mouth, skipped over to me, spread out her skirt and curtsied. Then she was allowed to stay with the rest of us and look on as the aunts came in. In the end, only Aunt Louise was left. Pappa had chosen her, but she kept going to the wrong person and getting snooks cocked at her, and each time she shrieked even louder and rushed out, waving her hands about to ward off the peals of laughter flying after her.

Then it was our turn to go out into the hall. The door was closed and you felt odder and odder the longer the silence in there lasted. Dr Montelius lit a cigar and Pappa started talking to a man I didn't know. I had to wait a long while before my turn came. Uncle Bori went in first, but he soon came back, and we heard the aunts in there laughing as he closed the door behind him.

Suddenly I was there in Aunt Malla's room, and everyone was looking at me in silence. A long time went by before my knees stopped shaking and I was able to find Nina among all those faces smiling expectantly at me. I looked down and walked quickly across the floor towards where Nina was sitting, bowed and scraped my foot. Then I looked up, about to sit down beside her, but noticed that all round me they were laughing. Nina had her fingers spread over her face, and she was also laughing.

'Wrong! Wrong!' cried Aunt Louise, slapping her knees.

I could make neither head nor tail of it all and tried to push aside a knee to get there, but then I saw that Nina really was cocking a snook at me. She turned her face and hands in my direction like a weather-vane and the splayed little finger was pointing straight at me. Someone took my arm, pointed at the door and told me to go out. Then I suddenly realized that Nina hadn't chosen me at all and they were laughing at me.

Then the game was no longer any fun. I tried with Aunt Malla, but she also cocked a snook at me, and now everyone had just as much fun as the time when she was standing in front of me. Bernt went in and stayed there. Once, I bowed in front of Uncle Bori, but then they all laughed even more than before and said it couldn't be an uncle. Every time I was made to feel more and more ashamed and the laughter sounded nastier and nastier. Cock-a-Snook was a loathsome game, the whole idea just to make a fool of me. And it was all Nina's fault.

In the end only Dr Montelius and I were left in the hall. He sucked on his cigar so that it glowed like a blood-red eye, and when he took his hand away it looked as if he had written some peculiar fiery letters in the air. Suddenly he put his hand on my shoulder, leant down and whispered: 'Try Mamma!'

The others were already sitting there looking at me. But they were no longer smiling, and they seemed to have become bored with my constant mistakes and had laughed long enough. Mamma was looking at me steadily straight in the eyes and there was a smile in the corner of her mouth. I could feel her eyes drawing me to her and guiding my steps over to her place. I bowed, Mamma inclined her head slightly and said: 'Yes!' Then she lifted me up on to her lap, kissed my cheek and pressed me to her. They all laughed, but they didn't look friendly and pleased any longer as if glad a happy event had at last occurred. I suddenly realized that of course Mamma would choose me in this game. Why hadn't this crossed my mind before?

'But Nina?' I said, shifting to a more comfortable position on Mamma's lap. 'Did she choose Aunt Paula?'

'No,' said Mamma. 'Nina chose Bernt.'

Then I saw Bernt was standing beside Nina's chair and had put his arm behind her along the back of the chair. Nina was looking up at him and saying something, and when she leant back, her hair swept over his arm.

22

WE ALL WENT OUT FOR A WALK IN THE EVENING. THE ROSE garden was veiled in mist, it was cool and moist, and when you ran through the grass it chilled your ankles and your sandals got dark and squelched when you put your foot down.

Mamma called out to me to stop spoiling my sandals, but I couldn't be bothered to obey. I was feeling odd and just wanted to do silly things. I leapt around and danced, thrashing my arms about and sticking my tongue out so that everyone could look at me. In passing, I tore leaves off rose-bushes and ripped them up, threw a stone at a bird and rushed several times at the girls from behind, trying to knock them down. Pappa shouted something in a loud voice, but I pretended not to hear and rushed away again, laughing, because everything I did seemed to me remarkable and very funny. Sometimes I stumbled and had to bend double to catch my breath, because I just couldn't stop laughing. Nina's eyes glittered inquisitively, full of excitement, so when I did anything really silly, she burst out laughing and pointed at me. But she kept at a distance the whole time, and joined Bernt and Katinka, as if she were afraid of me.

I had pretended to be blind for a long while, spinning round on the path with my eyes tight shut, so that in the end I landed at the feet of the grown-ups and butted Aunt Malla in the stomach. When I looked around, I noticed the others had run away from me and were far down at the other end of the avenue, looking at something lying at their feet. I stuck my tongue under my lower lip, rolled my eyes and approached them, swinging my arms and legs like a jumping Jack. But they didn't even turn their heads when I let out a shrill crowing sound behind them.

'Just look how fat it is!' said Katinka.

At first I thought it was a rat or a rabbit sitting on the gravel at their feet. But then I saw it was a gigantic toad. I had never seen such a huge one before. She took a few clumsy jumps, plumped down on her broad, flat belly and went rigid, as if too lazy to move any further, only the slimy, knobbly skin behind her cheeks pulsating as if she were panting from the effort. Then she turned her protruding yellow eye in my direction and glared distrustfully and dopily at me.

'Greetings, Queen Toad!' I cried, bowing low.

The toad slowly closed her eye and opened it, but didn't answer.

I filled my mouth with spit and dropped a white blob on to her back.

'Don't,' said Bernt. 'That's not funny at all.'

The toad moved slightly, turned half-way round and then stiffened again with her elbows up and fingers splayed out on the gravel. She didn't even try to clean herself.

'Oooh!' shrieked Nina, leaping back. 'It's trying to get me.'

'You've gone and annoyed it,' said Katinka. 'It might squirt poison at us all.'

Again we stood there without moving, just looking.

'How ugly it is,' exclaimed Nina. 'Look at those warts on its back and on the skin under its chin! Do any of you dare touch it?'

'Or catch it?' said Katinka. 'Ugh, I go goosy all over just looking at it.'

'Oh, that's nothing,' I said contemptuously. 'Here's someone who's not afraid!'

I don't know how I dared, but I suppose it was because everything seemed so peculiar and I thought it didn't matter what I did. It was like picking up a dark-brown, wrinkled leather pouch with something slimy and heavy inside. It kept kicking all the time and scratching my palms, slippery little hands sliding out and waving in the air.

'Look!' I cried. 'What a stomach!'

But the others had retreated and were looking at me in horror.

'Throw it away!' shrieked Katinka. 'You'll get warts on your hands.'

I went over to Nina, but her eyes widened with terror and she screamed. At once I knew what I had wanted to do all evening. I rushed at her. She turned round and fled, but just before she got to the grown-ups, she tripped, fell and rolled over. I threw the toad and it hit her right in the face with a disgusting smacking sound.

The grown-ups surrounded me. Nina was howling and Aunt Paula was wiping her face with her handkerchief.

'Now this has gone too far,' said Aunt Paula in a loud voice, red patches appearing on her cheeks and neck. 'Throwing a toad in someone's face! That can give you cramp!

'Just look at your dress, oh, dear, dear me,' lamented Aunt Louise, rocking to and fro with her hands clasped and her head back.

Suddenly Pappa was standing in front of me, his eyes flashing. He grabbed me by the arm. 'Is that the way to play with girls?' he said. 'Haven't I taught you to be chivalrous?'

I went stiff all over and could only feel him squeezing my arm.

'Chivalrous!' repeated Pappa. 'But what do you do? Put your mother and me to shame all evening.' His voice shook, and I thought, now the worst is to come.

'Go straight to Aunt Paula and Nina and apologize. Well, what about it?' He squeezed my arm even harder. 'Answer me!'

I leant back as far as I could, pressed my lips together and shook my head.

'Hooligan!' said Pappa and struck me across the back

of my neck with the side of his hand. It didn't hurt particularly, although it felt as if my head would fly off. I started crying and could see nothing more.

But it was horrid of Pappa to insult me and hit me while everyone was looking on, and at the same time talk about chivalry. Why did I have to be nice to Nina, who did nothing but tease me? And why weren't you allowed to joke with girls and frighten them in the same way as boys when you're playing with them?

23

'I KNOW SOMETHING! I KNOW!' CRIED NINA, LOOKING teasingly at me.

'What do you know?' I said, trying to hold her hand.

But she pulled hers away and ran over to Bernt and Katinka, who were by the fence. Bernt was peeling an osier with a penknife for the girls.

'Won't tell you!' Nina spread out her skipping-rope and skipped up and down beside Katinka as the rope swung round, occasionally turning to face Katinka and bursting into tinkling laughter.

We had been reconciled and all was well again. We had played with the dolls, Nina had said I was her husband and we were to be married when we grew up. But now she had started teasing me again.

'I don't care what you know,' I said with annoyance, stopping a few steps away from her.

Nina went on skipping and swinging the rope round. She seemed to be flying through the air, her dress and hair fluttering around her, arms out, knees pressed together and the toes of her small red sandals pointing downwards

– just like in the picture of the girl in the red shoes in our story book. 'I know,' she cried. 'Shall I tell you, Katinka?'

She stumbled, stopped and grabbed at Katinka to keep her balance. Katinka leant down and whispered in her ear for ages. Nina stared mockingly at me. 'I'll say it anyhow!' she cried.

She started skipping again, the rope spinning round so quickly she seemed to be inside a gigantic, glittering circle.

'There are. . .!' she sang. 'There are . . . other nice boys besides Riki!'

'Stop it!' said Katinka, pulling at her arm.

But Nina took a great hop to one side and went on singing:

'Kotik and Borja
Borja and Aljoscha
Aljoscha and Kotik . . .

'Oh, I can't do any more.' She tripped on the rope again. 'Do you remember Kotik's golden duck, Katinka? And Aljoscha – he had great shiny eyes, much more beautiful than Riki's.' She looked me straight in the eye and laughed. 'Do you remember, Katinka, how we got married in Pappa's study under his desk? And you were the priest and had taken the bedspread off Pappa's bed and wrapped it round you.'

Katinka put her hand over her mouth to stop herself bursting out laughing.

'But you couldn't marry that Aljoscha,' I yelled angrily. 'Because you're my wife. You said so yourself.'

'Of course I'm married to Aljoscha – and to Kotik and Borja too. They were already there before you!'

'But you've promised to marry me properly when we're grown up.'

'Of course I'll marry you. But I'll have the other boys I've promised as well. I'll marry them all. Kotik and Borja and Aljoscha and Bernt and you . . .'

'You're lying!' I screamed. 'You can't have more than one husband when you're a grown-up.' I swung round on my heel and walked away.

But Nina had picked up the skipping-rope and was skipping up and down on the lawn like a rubber ball. I heard her singing behind me:

'Kotik and Borja,
Borja and Aljoscha,
Aljoscha, Borja, Kotik –
They danced and skipped,
they skipped and hopped,
they hopped and danced –
and married me!'

24

KATKINKA HAD A WREATH OF YELLOW WATER-LILIES IN HER hair. 'Look,' she said. 'Don't I look like a mermaid? Bernt picked them for me.'

I at once said I would pick one for Nina. But the water-lilies were so far out I couldn't reach them, although I waded out into the water with my trousers rolled up. 'How did you pick them?' I asked.

Bernt pointed at a row of stones rising out of the water. 'You can get there if you jump from one stone to the next. But it's not worth your trying. You can't jump that far.'

'Of course I can,' I said.

'You're too small and you'd fall in the lake. Then Mamma will be cross with me for not keeping an eye on you.'

'Of course I can,' I persisted.

'No, you stay on the shore. I'd rather go out again and pick some for Nina.'

Before Bernt could stop me, I had rushed away from him and waded out towards the stones.

'Don't blame me, then!' cried Bernt. 'I'll tell Mamma.'

'Same to you, sneak!' I yelled back.

The water came right up to my thighs and wet the bottom of my trousers, but I got on to the first stones without much difficulty. Then it was easy to stride from stone to stone. My feet left dark footprints on the smooth, warm surface. But it was still a long way to the water-lilies, and a wide stretch of water now separated me from the next stone. At first I thought I'd jump, but when I saw how far it was, I was frightened, so I squatted down and stretched out one foot as far as I could to see if it reached the stone. But it didn't.

'You see!' cried Bernt. 'Now do as you're told and come back at once!'

'Come away from there!' called Katinka. 'Nina can borrow my wreath.'

'Do as Bernt says,' cried Nina. 'I don't mind about the flowers.'

Without thinking, I jumped. Somehow or other I landed on the other side and clung on to the stone with my fingers and toes. But one foot slipped and sank for a moment into the water so that it splashed all round me. 'You see!' I yelled. 'I know better than Bernt.'

Bernt's face appeared behind the stones. I had to hurry. I jumped several times and succeeded in landing again. I had already reached the water-lilies and a really fine one was nodding at me on its thick, juicy stalk. I squatted down and reached out for it. But I couldn't reach it.

Suddenly I felt myself falling. One moment I could still see the water-lily and the ripple of waves below me, then something hit me in the face and everything turned glowing white and I could feel the water closing in over me.

Then I was standing on the shore, water pouring off my clothes, out of my nose and mouth, and my eyes were smarting. My ears seemed to be blocked with cotton wool – I saw the others opening their mouths and staring at me, their eyes wide with fright. Their cries slowly reached me, apparently from far away.

'Run! Run!'

I started running. They ran ahead of me, shrieking with joy so that it echoed all over the garden.

'Mamma! Aunt Paula! Aunt Louise! Riki's fallen in the lake! He's fallen in the water!'

Then I was in the salon where the grown-ups were sitting. I ignored all their astonished, amused or annoyed expressions, and Popotjka's malicious screeches. They didn't matter. Everything was wet and horrible, water dripping and running off me everywhere, a large pool spreading over the parquet floor where I was standing. I was shaking with cold and trying to hold my elbows out as far as possible because it felt so horrible touching myself.

Mamma quickly put down her knitting and led me off to Aunt Louise's room. Then I stood in front of Aunt Louise, her fingers shaking as she pulled and tugged at my clothes and peeled them off me. They were sticking to my skin like a cold compress. 'Stand still!' she shrieked, pushing her armchair straight. 'That's nothing to be ashamed of.'

'And you had on a clean blouse and trousers when we left home,' said Mamma reproachfully.

My clothes looked dreadful, and only then did I notice they were covered with mud and green algae. I bent down and tried to remove the sea-grass that had wound itself round my knee.

'Stand still!' shrieked Aunt Louise, shaking me by the shoulders. 'Do you think I don't know what a naked boy looks like? Do you think I've never seen a naked boy in my life before, eh?'

Her whole crumpled little face was shaking with annoyance. I didn't understand why she was shrieking like that. I'm sure she knows perfectly well what naked boys look like. For they all look alike, Bernt and the workers' boys and little Tommy and even the little angels with no clothes on in Grandmother's book. And there's nothing special about them, although they've got such little willies, but perhaps Aunt Louise's is much bigger. I was shivering only because I was cold and because Aunt Louise's hands were so wrinkled and knobbly and covered with hideous veins and were shaking so it tickled. I couldn't make out why Aunt Louise kept on shrieking about that and looked so angry. In the end I felt ashamed of myself and thought there must be something nasty about me Aunt Louise probably knew about, but I myself didn't understand.

'Here's the towel,' said Mamma, wrapping it round me. 'Rub him really hard to get him warm, while I wash his knees and feet.'

'Yes, good gracious, he might get pneumonia. Don't wriggle like that, do you hear?'

Aunt Louise is much more heavy-handed than Mamma is, and she rubbed and scoured me as if with a scrubbing-brush, twisting and turning me as if I were just an object. When she dried between my legs, it felt as if she were about to claw and tear away everything there, so I screamed Ow! and had to hop on one leg. But it was better then anyhow, now that she couldn't touch my bare skin.

'What shall we put him in so that he doesn't catch cold?' said Mamma, collecting up the sticky heap of clothes lying on the floor. 'Wait here on the bed and keep the towel round you.'

Mamma and Aunt Louise went out. After a while, I heard them talking in the next room. I could make out Popotjka's voice, too – he was chattering and talking without stopping, occasionally interrupting the others with reproving screeches.

'That's nothing,' I heard Aunt Paula's voice saying. 'He can borrow Nina's dress.'

'Mamma!' I shouted, jerking open the door. 'I won't put on Nina's dress. Whatever you do, you can't make me.'

'Nina's dress!' persisted Popotjka. 'Nina's dress.'

'Don't shout,' said Mamma. 'There aren't any other dry clothes in the house.'

'But I don't want to. They'll laugh at me.'

'No one will laugh at you. What's so strange about putting on a dress? As if girls don't often go around in boy's clothes.'

But Mamma was smiling and looking meaningfully at Aunt Louise, whose toothless mouth was grinning broadly. Aunt Paula bit her lip and exchanged a look of understanding with the others. Popotjka winked back with one eye, then closed both eyes with an innocent look as if he had fallen asleep on his steel ring and was quite unaware of anything. They were all thinking about something funny and ridiculous they would soon be showing to the others. Then I saw the heads of Katinka, Nina and Bernt appearing in the doorway opposite. I wrapped the towel more firmly round me and gave them a challenging look.

'One moment,' said Aunt Paula. 'I'll be back soon.'

'It isn't at all the same! Boys . . . girls. . . !'

My knees were shaking, my heart thumping and my tongue wouldn't do what it was told. I couldn't get out what I wanted to say.

'Of course it's the same,' said Mamma. 'It's just the same if a boy wears girl's clothes or a girl wears boy's.'

'No, it's not true! You're lying!' I yelled.

For Mamma really was lying and it wasn't at all true it was just the same.

'Don't be rude,' said Mamma. 'You've already been naughty enough today. Bernt has told me what happened. Now be quiet and do as you're told.'

'Do as you're told!' repeated Popotjka, sticking his

head out through the bars. He raised his crest and showered me with threats and ignominious invective in cockatoo language.

'Here it is,' said Aunt Paula, holding the dress up with a smile. It was the same blue dress Nina had had on the first time we met. 'Now please stop making such a fuss. You're a sensible boy. Come and put it on, now, then it's over and done with. One, two, three!' coaxed Aunt Paula.

Horrified, I looked from one to the other, but they were all against me. They were big and strong and I alone was small and weak. Oh, if only I was a magician! I should have annihilated them with a look, or turned myself into a tiger and torn them to shreds. But I couldn't. The end had come. 'You mustn't!' I screamed. 'You mustn't! I'll kill you all!'

I rushed out into the back room and threw myself howling on to the floor. I wrapped the towel round me as hard as I could. Mamma and Aunt Paula tried to jerk it off me and pull the dress over my head, but they couldn't. I kicked and rolled about on the floor, holding on to the towel with my hands and teeth as if it were my own skin.

'What an insufferable boy,' said Mamma. 'I'm going to fetch Uncle Bori. He'll probably get the better of you.'

Silence fell all round me. For a long time I heard nothing but my own sobs and gasps. When I had recovered sufficiently to look up, I saw Uncle Bori's expressionless face in the doorway, his pince-nez flashing so that I couldn't make out whether he was smiling or looking sternly at me. But the thought of his having seen my shame and heard my howls made me stop. I jumped up, let the towel fall, raised my arms and dived into the dress Aunt Paula was pulling over my head. I didn't dare look at the door in case Uncle Bori came in. For that would have been worse than having to wear girl's clothes.

They all smiled when I came into the salon. My cheeks were burning and I couldn't look anyone in the eye. The blue dress hung down in the front and spread out like an apron. I saw my brown arms and legs sticking out of it, but they didn't seem to belong to me at all and I didn't know how to move them.

I rushed off to another room, because I didn't want to go out and play with the others so that Crane and the horses would see me and laugh. It was more than enough that Popotjka had witnessed everything and screeched it out in cockatoo language, making it echo all over the house.

Nina came running after me. 'Now we look just the same!' she cried, clapping her hands. Her laugh wasn't at all unkind and I was also beginning to think the whole affair was rather amusing. 'Look!' she said, leading me over to a mirror. 'It's true, isn't it? We're like two sisters.'

There was indeed a strange girl in the mirror, holding Nina's hand. They looked alike, the same height and with almost the same dresses. But one of them had my face and tearful, red-rimmed eyes.

'Come on,' said Nina. 'We'll go up to our room and play with the dolls. We can both be mothers now.'

Nina lent me half of the dolls and so I was mamma and had a whole lot of children of my own. It wasn't much fun. At first Nina kept scolding me because I was so clumsy when I was going to cook food for the dolls and feed them. But gradually I got more interested in the game and had almost forgotten the dress when Mamma called us and said we must go home.

Now the misery began all over again. I didn't mind that much about the workers' boys fishing on the shore, because they thought it was a girl in the boat as we rowed past. But there was worse to come. I wrapped the towel round me so the dress wouldn't show and kept close behind Mamma. But everyone already knew. When we got to the Heavenly Staircase, Aunt Leli and Aunt Else were on the terrace, laughing and questioning Mamma. Uncle Frans got out of his reclining chair on the balcony and looked down. Aunt Sonja's lace cap could just be seen in the window and the ordinary Aunt Lotte was leaning over the balcony rail at Aunt Luscha's house. When we went on, both the big and the little Aunt Lala, and Aunt Dulla and Uncle Bobbi and lovely Karin were coming to meet us. Mamma stopped and had to tell them everything. And Uncle Georg came out of the woodshed and he, too, stopped to listen.

'However could you be so careless!' said big Aunt Lala, shaking her head.

Aunt Dulla twirled her parasol and peered at me, and lovely Karin cried out 'Show us! Show us!' and lifted up the towel so that the blue shone below.

And all three Falkenheimer aunts called out from their veranda: 'Vot a deelightful leetle girrl!'

As we went on, the cows all lowed, the ducks quacked, the geese stretched out their necks, hissing at me and trying to jerk away the towel I had round me. And Uncle Erni's rooster with his golden brown breast and green tail-feathers flew up off the rubbish-heap, flapping his wings and crowing.

'I'm *not* a girl!' I shouted, feeling the tears coming. 'I'm a marabou stork! Can't you see?'

They should all have noticed that I was like a marabou stork when I was folded into the fluffy white towel, so my arms didn't show and only my neck and legs stuck out. And behind me was a white train, just like a bird's tail.

That evening, Aunt let me run out into the garden and play for a while before I went to bed. It was already chilly, the air yellow and thick, the shadows long and mosquitoes hovering in the air in golden clouds.

While I'm running about out there on the soft lawn, my feeling of sorrow and shame quickly fades away. It is lovely to skip and dance and let the dress flutter, to let the evening wind blow up it like a curtain and stroke and caress my body. It's like dancing in nothing but my shirt out on the grass and as if the whole world were my bed, the trees and stones, the house with all its windows and the horses grazing in the meadow far away, looking on.

When I squat down by a flower and lower my head, I suddenly notice that everything shows under there. I look at my willie and it looks back at me. It's like a little elephant and looks so pleased, just as if it were laughing and wanted to call out something to me.

Willie, I think, and feel a mysterious sense of pride and happiness tight in my chest. Willie!

I go on skipping and dancing and feel the dress turning into something wonderful, as if it were a magic cloak. Never, not even when Mamma or Aunt has taken me in her arms, have I been caressed as I am by this dress, so softly and kindly, as it now glides over my body and encloses it in all directions. It flutters and flaps, it lifts me up and I feel I'm as light as a feather.

It is no longer the dress – someone is whirling round with me, stroking me and floating away with me in their arms. And now the trees and the stones are also dancing round us, the house leaping up and down, the forest and fields standing on end and the horses swaying like a see-saw. The whole world is dancing with us. But then I can't manage any more and fling myself gasping down on the grass.

25

IT WAS AUNT LOUISE'S NAME-DAY. WHEN WE CAME IN, THE salon was seething with innumerable aunts and uncles I'd never seen before and I had to go round shaking hands and bowing to them all.

But I recognized Oliver immediately. The sunlight

coming in through the tall windows was flickering in the leaves of the palms and myrtle-bushes, making him look all silvery as he stood in the middle of the floor, dazzling spots of sunlight reflected from the chandelier falling on his black velvet jacket and glimmering on his forehead as if he were wearing a diadem. He smiled at me and flicked me lightly and intimately on the head. I was so confused and pleased, I couldn't take in what he was saying. But I took his touch to be a kind of ceremony by which he had marked me out from the others.

When Aunt Gulla tried to left me up on to her lap, I was furious. Naturally I wanted to sit on Oliver's lap, and I soon managed to wriggle free and run over to him. He helped me up and let me bounce up and down on his knees. That was quite different from the loose, unsteady arms of the aunts. He took me in his firm hands and threw me high up into the air and then caught me again. I screamed with terror and delight as I flew over the chandeliers above everyone's heads.

Bernt and the girls were looking on, disappointed and envious, then they crowded round Oliver demanding that he should do the same to them. But at that moment, Aunt Louise said dinner was served and everyone got up and headed for the door. I found myself squashed between Aunt Paula's soft, bouncy hips and fat Uncle Erni's huge stomach, so I couldn't see a thing.

When everyone was seated at the table, to my dismay I found we were separated. Oliver was sitting right down at the other end of the table, talking and joking with an almost grown-up girl. She had thick plaits and a pink hair-ribbon and I wished her to blazes. Oliver's way of wrinkling his eyebrows and then letting his face broaden into a bright smile made me completely forget about the food. His eyes are very large and full of dark reflections when he opens them wide and lets them roam round the company.

Aunt Louise asked me why I didn't like the duck, and Mamma, sitting beside me, pulled my arm several times and told me to hurry up. But I hardly got a bite down although it was so exciting eating duck. I turned the tough meat over in my mouth, but it got drier every minute and my jaws ached. Long after the others had finished their dessert, I was still sitting with my plate half-full in front of me, swallowing and chewing and, ashamed, wondering what Oliver would think of me.

When I finally got down from the table, Nina came up to me and suggested we went out into the garden to play.

The dolls were missing their father, and all morning they had been so whiny and naughty Nina had undressed them completely and thrown them into the nettles. But that was only because they had been waiting so excitedly for me to come and had been rather awkward during my long absence. We were now going to take them on an outing to the rose garden. But I didn't feel like going with them and looked round for Oliver. He must have gone with the grown-ups into the music-room, and I could hear a murmur of talk and laughter and see wisps of blue smoke coming from there.

Nina at first thought I was joking or in a bad temper. She took my arm and pulled me towards the veranda door. But when I resisted and she couldn't get me to move, the teasing sparkle in her eyes faded away. 'Why are you being like this?' she cried. 'Why don't you want to come out and play?'

'Because,' I said, trying to avoid her eyes. 'Just because. I'm tired and I think it's boring. Let's go to the music-room instead and see who's playing.'

Nina jerked my arm so roughly, I stumbled quite a way into the room before I managed to stop. 'Come on!' she shrieked 'You must come! You must!'

She kept her head down so that her face was hidden by her glossy golden hair, and she kept laughing as if the whole thing were a joke. But when she looked up for a moment, I saw that her face was quite red and her eyes full of tears.

'Let go!' I cried. 'You're hurting me.'

I meant to hit her, because my shoulder was hurting so, but she let go my arm, straightened up and pushed her hair off her forehead.

'Leave me alone!' I shouted, for I was really angry by then. 'I don't want to play with you, because you're only a girl. It's always the same. Pappa and Mamma. Toys – stoves and dolls! I'm fed up with it.'

Nina listened, her mouth clenched tight shut, her eyes flashing. Then she suddenly raised her hand and hit me. The blow struck my upper lip. I grabbed at her hair, but everything happened so quickly and unexpectedly she had time to rush down the veranda steps.

I howled, not so much from pain as from anger at Nina managing to run away before I had time to retaliate.

'Nina hit me! Nina hit me!' I stammered when Aunt Malla came rushing in to see what was going on.

'Stop that noise,' said Aunt Malla. 'They're playing in there.' She patted me, blew on my swollen lip and wiped my face with her handkerchief. Then she took my hand and led me into the room where the grown-ups were sitting. There was such an awful murmuring and roaring and rumbling in there, I hid my face in Aunt Malla's bosom in fright as she lifted me up, and I didn't dare turn round to look for quite a while. I had to keep blinking all the time, I was so afraid the palms and the myrtle-bushes would tip over and the pictures and mirrors crash to the floor. The grown-ups were lined up on chairs along the walls, their faces expressionless, except two old ladies whispering over in one corner. No one responded to my smiles, some of them staring ahead and frowning, others glassy-eyed and vacant. Oliver was sitting over by the window, where the light was trickling in through the white curtains, and his head was resting against his hand. His eyes were closed and he looked asleep, a strange expression of melancholy on his face I'd never noticed before, but which in my view made him look even more beautiful. I at once realized he looked just like the dark-haired angel who had always held such a mysterious attraction for me.

The music came to an end with a series of resounding thumps that sounded like cowbells, then died away into a dark underworld thunder. Everyone clapped and fat Uncle Erni got up behind the huge black wing of the grand piano with a drowsy smile and ran his handkerchief across his forehead. I laughed and clapped like the others, but there wasn't a sound when I banged my hands together.

'Interesting,' said Pappa, fixing his monocle behind the frame of his glasses. 'Very interesting.'

Aunt Louise yawned and waved her mantilla in front of her mouth. 'Dreadful! Muscha, dear, what do you think? Why can't he compose real music?'

'Original, anyhow!' said Kuno Grim, smiling so that all his teeth gleamed in his black beard.

Everyone started arguing and talking at the same time, Aunt Louise shrieking that music should be pure and beautiful, and others flatly disagreeing. Fat Uncle Erni thrust his hands into his jacket pockets and walked slowly out of the room. Aunt Louise said she was tired of all these frightful new-fangled pieces and asked Dr Montelius to play something decent, a romance or a waltz you could listen to without its setting your teeth on edge or giving you earache.

While Dr Montelius was playing and the younger aunts and uncles were swinging round the salon, I managed to run over to Oliver and crawl up on to his lap. I was allowed to feel his muscles and poke at his chin, mouth and eyelids. He squeezed his eyes tight shut and laughed. Then he leant over me and whispered with his mouth close to my ear that he would come and visit me on my birthday. It tickled my ear as if a butterfly had brushed past it.

When we went down to the boat, Katinka and Nina were at the bottom of the steps jumping up and down. 'Girlboy! Girlboy!' cried Nina, pointing at me.

But I took no notice of their horrid attempts to annoy me over that dress.

During the journey home, I was so full of Oliver I couldn't talk about anything else, and every time I closed my eyes I saw his face in front of me. But suddenly it wasn't Oliver's face, but the face of that dark, curly-haired angel I like looking at so much.

The following morning, I took the rainbow-coloured silk shawl Aunt had left lying over a chair in the nursery, put it round my shoulders and held it out with my hands like a pair of wings. I stretched up as far as I could, swung my arms to and fro, and danced in a ring round Tommy, holding my head slightly to one side as Oliver often does, peering round and trying to conjure up his image. When I kept on thinking hard about him, I really did manage to transform myself for a few moments so that his image merged with me. I was no longer me but Oliver dancing round the room and smiling at Tommy.

Tommy was crouched on the floor with some building bricks and following me with his eyes, dumb with admiration and astonishment. But then he scrambled up and trotted after me with his arms out. That made me angry with him and I smacked him. His heart-rending cries brought Aunt rushing in. She started scolding me, snatched her shawl away and comforted Tommy. But it was obvious he had no right to try to be Oliver, for Oliver belongs to me. I'm the one who has sat on his lap and it's my angel he resembles.

My birthday was one of the happiest days of my life. I was allowed to put on my white sailor suit with long trousers, and Aunt did my hair in front of the mirror, with a parting on one side. I thought I looked really nice and waited with excitement for Oliver to come in and see me.

Oliver came with the other guests, bent down and lifted me up in his arms. I was so pleased to see him again, I kissed him. He handed me a little bottle and a thin tube wrapped in tissue paper. I must have looked rather disappointed, because I didn't know how to play with them.

'It's only a trifle,' said Oliver. 'But you can do lovely conjuring tricks with them.' He undid the tissue paper, uncorked the bottle, dipped the silver tube into the yellowish fluid and pulled it out again. 'Watch now,' he said.

And at that moment a tiny little silvery ball appeared on the end of the tube. It swelled and trembled and grew thinner and thinner and more and more transparent as if it consisted of glittering crystal. Soon it was as big as an orange, shimmering in green, dark red and blue. The curved rainbow surface spun round, and inside it appeared a reduced picture of the windows, the sky and the sunny garden outside. Quite soundlessly, the bubble freed itself from the tube and floated slowly past me. I seized it in my hand, but it immediately disappeared. Oliver at once conjured up some more bubbles, which slowly floated up to the ceiling. I'd never seen anything so beautiful. Sometimes, a whole cloud of bubbles came out of the tube, some as big and brilliant as peacock's feathers, others small and gleaming metallically in gold, pink and sky-blue. The room was soon full of this shower of wonderful coloured spheres rising and falling past each other, getting stuck on lampshades, brushing the aunts' hair and then suddenly, quite unexpectedly being obliterated just when they were glittering at their very best and clearest.

But the best part of my birthday was that I was allowed to stay up for the evening when the grown-ups had tea, and I was allowed to decide who should sit next to me. Of course I chose Oliver. That was the high point of the party, and the feeling of being totally in possession of Oliver made me tired and drowsy. As soon as I looked up from my cup to ensure he was still sitting next to me, I saw a huge pair of golden wings had grown out of his shoulders. His suit glinted gold and silver, he had a diadem round his forehead and his eyes were sparkling so brightly I was afraid. But he was looking kindly at me, put his arm round my shoulders and pulled me to him, the huge golden wing shading me like a parasol. The guests were seething round us and a shower of gleaming bubbles floated silently through the room. Happy and tired, I collapsed on to Oliver's chest and fell asleep.

26

KATINKA AND NINA HAD GONE AWAY WITH THEIR PARENTS, but Oliver was still at Salmela.

We walk hand in hand down to the pasture to look at Aunt Louise's carriage horses. They are long-legged, slender animals with trembling, velvety hides, white rings round their hocks and a white patch on their cheeks that looks like an eye. At a distance, it makes their faces look horribly dangerous, like a man-eater's. These horses are very old, too, and presumably originally came from General Grund's flying team. Now they are standing quite still beside each other, shoulder to shoulder, their lower lips hanging with a tired and bitter expression as they ill-humouredly nose at the grass. Aunt Louise has long since stopped riding in her carriage because she doesn't want to tire the horses. They never have to do anything but stay in the pasture or the stable and take a little exercise now and again.

Sometimes I stand by the bridge and look on while Oliver and some of the farm men – all mounted – appear on the opposite shore and drive the horses down into the lake. Oliver is wearing bathing-trunks but the labourers are quite naked. The horses shy, but then dance playfully sideways down into the water, the riders clinging hard with their thighs to stay on. After the animals have waded a little way out, they dip their necks down into the water and then glide forward softly and quickly, their eyes wide open with anxiety as they snort wildly and impatiently, shooting their heads and necks forward in a beautiful arch. Their manes flutter like sea-grass and it looks as if they are being carried along on a wave. The riders are towed through the water, holding on to the manes or the reins, their extended bodies gleaming, pale and unclear in the dark swirl. When the horses reach the bottom, they thrust up their swanlike necks, as if their bodies curled after them like sea-serpents. They don't regain their real shape until the riders are once again on their backs and the animals' dark bodies rise noisily out of the water.

Oliver reins in his horse, which lowers its head and snorts as it champs at its bit. He shouts something to me that I don't catch. Water is pouring off the horse's darkening coat in a silver stream as well as off Oliver's knees and heels, and is dripping from his hair. His back and shoulders gleam in the evening sun as if they were of copper. He sits high up, almost as if he were banging his head against the golden cloud floating above him.

'Take me with you! Take me with you!' I shout, stretching my arms out imploringly.

But Oliver laughs, waves his hand and suddenly floats away on his horse, a few cold drops of water splashing my face all that is left of him.

I rush after him, fall over on the road, scramble up again and rush on, though my knee stings like fire and dark drops of blood ooze out between the lumps of dirt stuck to it. But Oliver is nowhere to be seen and I open my mouth and howl, airing all my grief and disappointment.

When I get back, Aunt Louise is standing by the window seething with fury. Her hands are shaking, her shell-like coiffure is in disorder and a few white strands stand straight up in the air like Popotjka's crest when he's angry. 'Right under my window!' she shrieks angrily. 'And no bathing-trunks on either! Such lecherous men!'

When we're having tea later on, Aunt Louise's hand is still shaking so badly tea splashes all over the tablecloth. Again and again, she utters a piercing screech: 'How disgusting! Vile! Ugh!'

'You schouldn't let Oliver be together with the labourer boysch scho much, madame,' says Kuno Grim, polishing his glasses with his handkerchief. 'They're not shuitable company for him and he might get up to all kindsch of basschnesh.' He adjusts his spectacles on his nose and hooks the sides behind his ears. 'It would be a mischfortschune, a treadful mischfortschune,' he says in a stifled voice, but then goes on in French.

Oliver appears on the veranda after a while, his shirt unbuttoned, his mouth half open, and he keeps pushing his wet hair back off his forehead. To me, he seems strange and new and so beautiful I'm afraid and ashamed and don't dare go near him. But he smiles intimately and lifts me up on to his lap. He is wet and cold, as if the wind were still blowing round him after his swift ride, and as if he had recently been galloping up among the clouds, floating through the endless blue space past the sun and the stars. 'What have you got there?' he says, looking at my badly grazed knee, which Aunt Malla has just washed and painted with iodine.

'Nothing much,' I say, feeling the tears coming back again. 'It was because you wouldn't take me with you. I ran after you and fell over.'

27

KUNO GRIM IS OFTEN SITTING ON THE VERANDA WHEN WE GO to visit the aunts, because his villa is over in the forest on the other side of the rose garden. I disliked him from the very first moment.

That long, dark-brown beard which almost completely hides his face, those dark sun-glasses, his pale-yellow straw hat with a black hatband – they all seem mysterious and frightening. When he is out walking, he swings a thin bamboo cane in his hand and his movements are dignified and deliberate. At every step he turns his toes outwards with an exquisitely elegant movement. He often leans thoughtfully on his stick, staring ahead of him as if working out the most suitable place for his toe at the next step. His voice is deep and purring, and when he speaks he runs his hand over his beard as if caressing it. He pouts his moist, red lips in a peculiar way and hisses like a snake. He says schocks and schugar and verry shad shircumstansches. When he's eating, bits of carrot and drops of sauce stick in his beard and he has to take his table-napkin, spread it out like a towel and wipe his face for ages, as if washing. His fingers and the backs of his hands are covered with dark hairs. He is sure to be hairy all over like an ape and has dressed up as a human being just to deceive us.

Although I prefer to keep Kuno Grim at a distance, I have to be in his company because Oliver is with him so much. It's clear that Kuno Grim makes a dead set at Oliver and often puts his pale, hairy hand protectively on Oliver's shoulder. They walk beside each other in the rose garden, Kuno Grim from time to time thoughtfully kicking at the end of his stick while Oliver describes something to him with lively gestures. Sometimes I sit for hours on the veranda listening dejectedly to their conversation, not a word of which I understand. Oliver easily gets excited, talking loudly and brushing his hair from his forehead. Kuno Grim blows long blue jets of smoke through his nostrils and out of his mouth and swings his foot up and down.

One day I followed them up the pine-covered sandy ridge to Kuno Grim's villa.

As soon as we had stepped into the dim light between the trees, an indescribable stench struck us. We went over to a high plank fence topped with barbed wire.

Quite suddenly, something began to howl and rush back and forth inside there, but neither Oliver nor Kuno Grim appeared to take much notice. They just went on towards the furious howl, although I cautiously tugged at Oliver's sleeve to make him turn back. When I finally stopped, uncertain whether to go on any longer, Kuno Grim looked searchingly at me and asked me if I was afraid. Of course I said no, and then I just had to put a bold face on it.

When Kuno Grim had suddenly disappeared somewhere, Oliver explained that there were silver foxes inside and we would soon be allowed to have a look at them.

Kuno Grim came back after a while with a swarthy, unshaven man with thick red lips, carrying a large rusty key in his hand. My heart was thumping wildly as he unlocked a creaking gate and we went in.

Two huge monsters, black and as horrible as wolves, rushed at us, snarling and menacingly swinging their heavy, hairy heads, their tongues now and again flaring like flames in their open mouths. Trembling, I pressed against Oliver, but when one of them lowered its head and, growling, sniffed at my leg, I could no longer control myself. I flew up and clung screaming round Oliver's neck. The monster let out a furious bark and leapt up at Oliver's chest, its jaws snapping just by my ankle.

The swarthy man had to grab its collar and strike it with his whip several times before it stopped trying to drag me down, all the time barking furiously and demanding that I should be handed over to it.

'Schtop making the dogsch nervousch,' hissed Kuno Grim, and the keeper said nastily: 'If you're no more of a man than that, then the dogs'll soon make a meal of you. They don't like you being afraid of them.'

'Why frighten him?' said Oliver, heaving me up so that I was sitting astride his shoulders. 'Don't be afraid. No one's going to eat you!'

The silver foxes themselves were a disappointment. They weren't silver at all and their fur was coming out in great chunks. They were either sitting or half lying quite still behind the bars of their cages, staring without blinking at me with their big yellow eyes. When we approached, they crouched down guiltily and slid swiftly off into their wooden cabins. The floors of the cages were spotted with blood, and fish skeletons, gnawed bones and corpses of small beheaded animals were lying about everywhere. A bitten-off head of a rabbit stared at me with shattered eyes. The stench all round us was indescribable and blue-and-green blowflies were buzzing everywhere.

Kuno Grim was walking ahead of us and said we must go quietly and not talk loudly, otherwise we would frighten the foxes and they would eat their young. He pointed at a thin fox crouched up on the roof of its cabin listening to our conversation with inquisitively pricked ears and impassive eyes.

'The day before yeschterday that schilver fox ate up all her cubsch before they'd even got hair on their bodiesch or opened their eyesch.'

I didn't like the silver foxes at all and wished I hadn't gone with Oliver. The puzzling silence of the foxes, their malicious, glowing eyes observing us from all directions and then becoming invisible as soon as we approached – it all seemed ghostly. Those mute, shadowy creatures imprisoned in there made me think of evil spirits and ghosts, although Kuno Grim persisted in calling them silver foxes. We were also at the foot of the Fire Mountain, where the Archangel had fought his battle with the spirits of hell.

After we had seen everything, we went up to Kuno Grim's villa just behind the enclosure containing the foxes' cages. The house was built of ugly, unpainted timbers and the window-panes glinted in the same gloomy way as Kuno Grim's glasses.

But inside it was strangely light, tiny golden grains of dust dancing in front of the window, the sunlight falling in broad, trembling streaks on the rug, the arms of the dark armchairs and the heavy oak table. The walls had shelves full of books and strange objects right up to the ceiling. Kuno Grim went over to a cupboard and pulled out a whole lot of flat drawers with glass lids, put them on the table and started explaining something to Oliver.

When I got closer, I cried out with delight. This was an even more beautiful display of colour than Aunt Louise's chandelier and the dazzling spots of sunlight on the walls in her salon.

The drawers were full of butterflies of all colours, their wings outspread – huge butterflies that appeared to be cut out of a piece of velvet, and little butterflies like silk bows or mother-of-pearl jewels. Some of them were decorated with gold and silver borders drawn by the brush of a painter of icons, others had dark rainbow spots on their wings gazing at me with solemn, velvety eyes.

But all the butterflies were quite still, fastened to the underlay with a pin. The pin ran right through their backs and chests like a spear and the butterflies were mounted on it, floating there in the drawer with their wings out, unable to rise or get free.

'Are they dead?' I said. 'Did they all die when they were speared through like that?'

'Yesch, of coursch,' said Kuno Grim. He took down a glass jar with something white at the bottom, unscrewed the lid and carefully tipped out a butterfly on to the palm of his hand. It was lying on its back with its legs helplessly pressed to its chest, its wings half closed like a moth. A strange sweet smell that tickled your nose and made your head heavy poured out of the jar.

'Thisch isch what I uschually do,' said Kuno Grim. He picked up the butterfly by the body between his finger and thumb and slowly stuck the pin through it. The butterfly's back curled up and it tried to spread out its wings. They were trembling slightly and glowing yellow and sky-blue in turn.

'It's alive!' I cried out.

'Schtoopid! It's schtone tead.'

He took a board down from the shelf and squeezed the butterfly into a crack dividing the board into two. Then he pulled out the wings and fastened them with a whole lot of thin pins he kept taking out of his mouth. The little butterfly was pinned down on the bench and could no longer move.

'It's schstone tead,' Kuno Grim repeated. 'It feelsch notting. That'sch notting but a reflexsch.'

I knew he was lying, because I'd just seen the little butterfly screaming for help as it felt the point of the needle going in. But butterflies have such thin, weak voices, ears can't hear them, only your mind can.

I left them. But it was no longer fun looking in the drawers. Poor butterflies! There was my friend the little green butterfly, and there were his brothers the Common Blues, and the little butterflies whose wings gleam so beautifully in gold and red – they used to play with me in the garden below our veranda. All of them had ended up here in Kuno Grim's awful black-edged drawer and were floating dead and unmoving under the glittering glass lid.

'Why do you kill them?' I asked finally.

'What a queschtion!' said Kuno Grim crossly. 'I collect butterfliesch. Look how lovely they are!'

After a while, we went out on to the veranda. Kuno Grim opened a huge book, drew his chair up next to Oliver's and turned the pages over. They were pictures of butterflies, nearly all of them as bright and beautiful as the ones I had just seen in the drawers. I grew sleepy and tired and would have liked to leave, because they just went on talking to each other. Kuno Grim took no notice of me, and Oliver also seemed to have forgotten I was there. He was sitting with his neck thrust out, looking in the book.

To kill time, I looked at Kuno Grim's face. It was funny to see the way his wrinkles slid back and forth on his forehead, the way his cheeks expanded and collapsed and his beard went up and down and shot out like a spade when he closed his mouth. Sometimes he twisted his mouth in a very peculiar way, his ears moving, then suddenly the brick-red gums and row of shiny white teeth shot forward out of his mouth like a crocodile. But he popped them back with his hand in horror, cleared his throat and licked his lips before going on talking.

'What does a Cossus look like?' Oliver asked him.

Kuno Grim put his fat white finger on a huge grey butterfly with magnificently patterned wings, as if cut out of a piece of bark. 'Coschusch, Coschusch!' he repeated, turning the dark lenses of his glasses on Oliver. And suddenly his face was distorted again in a strange way, his lips protruding like a snout. He hissed and fizzed so little drops of spit splashed my forehead. 'Coschusch! Coschuuuuuschsch!'

'Why do you talk so funnily, Uncle Kuno?' I said.

'What?' He fell silent and turned round. 'What did you schay?'

'Why do you say Coschusch, Coschusch like that?'

I did my best to twist up my face in the same way as he did, and to imitate his horrible hissing.

The next moment I found myself lying face down across Kuno Grim's knee. The whole room was upside-down, the floor about to tip over me. All I could see was the chair legs and the heels of Kuno Grim's shoes.

'What do you schay to thisch?' said a menacing, icy voice and a terrible heavy hand descended on my backside. 'And thisch and thisch!' the voice repeated. The blows came at regular intervals. I could almost calculate when the next one was going to fall and each time it smarted and hurt even more.

I clenched my teeth and held my breath, because I didn't want to cry. I didn't want to show that I minded. You just go on hitting, I thought. You won't make me cry anyhow. I can feel nothing. I can feel nothing.

He was already hitting me so hard I was just about to fall apart, my whole backside burning like fire, and after each blow his hand seem to dwell there for a while, as if enjoying the pain and burning under the seat of my trousers.

I can't feel anything. I can't feel anything! I can't feel anything. . . .

Suddenly he stopped. I was free and fled howling down the veranda steps. I could hear the wolfhounds throwing themselves at the fencing with furious barks as I rushed past. Terrified, I ran on, my knees giving way, my chest hurting as if something were about to burst inside it the very next moment. But I had to go on, for if I'd stopped, all that horror and evil behind me would catch up with me and all would be at an end.

28

IT WASN'T UNTIL I GOT TO THE ROSE GARDEN THAT I CAME to my senses and realized I was saved.

What should I do? After the terrible thing that had happened to me, I could never again show myself to anyone. None of them would ever like me again once they'd been told how Kuno Grim had shouted at me, put me over his knee and smacked my bottom. It was still burning and aching, and at the same time I didn't seem to have any backside left at all, so strange and stiff and numb it felt. Sometimes that hateful hand seemed to be still resting on my backside.

He would tell everyone how he had smacked me and how in the end I had started crying. They would all laugh and think it served me right because I'd been so rude. Worst of all was that Oliver had witnessed everything.

I crept sobbing along the stone wall to the arbour where I used to play with Nina, and I dived down under the lilacs. Great glittering drops were hanging from the ends of the leaves, one falling now and again and dripping with a slow plop down into the foliage. The bushes seemed to be crying with me. I curled up on the sandy floor of our abandoned play place and wiped away the snot and tears with my sleeve.

I was protected there. No one could see me. I would never again crawl out and join the others. They would have to run round the garden calling out to me, but I would keep quiet and not let them know I was quite close and could see and hear them. I wouldn't crawl out if they wept and pleaded with me to come back, promising me whole bags of toffee, crystallized fruit and chocolate.

A teaspoon Nina had forgotten when we were playing our games was sticking out of the sand, and one of the doll's blankets was lying dark and crumpled like a rag. A crowd of black ants crept out from under it, rushing uneasily back and forth across the sand and waving their antennae about. But they were too small to console me, so there was no point in saying anything to them.

I took a pinch of sand and let it trickle down on to the ants. They turned and fled in terror, like wanderers in the desert surprised by a sandstorm. One of the ants was buried under the sand and for a long time I watched it trying to free its trapped body and the way the grains of sand moved above the place where it had been completely covered.

To the ants, I was a giant, a god. Their lives and

destinies lay in my hard hands, and they were seized with mortal anguish at the sight of my terrible power. How could an ant I held between my thumb and finger understand that I had been hurt, and that I had recently been just as helpless and terrified in the hands of Kuno Grim?

It was quite quiet and still, the only sound the raindrops dripping in the lilacs and somewhere high up in the tree-tops a soughing and clicking of wet leaves. However long I waited, no footsteps or cries could be heard, and the whole garden lay there utterly abandoned and forgotten. No one had noticed I was missing. No one was searching for me or calling me back. Why didn't they come? Were they all so indifferent to me?

29

NIGHT HAS ALREADY FALLEN, AND I AM STILL CROUCHING under the lilac-bushes.

The darkness round me is so thick and black, I no longer know if my eyes are open or closed. Suddenly a winking star appears far away, then gets bigger and bigger and shines with an increasingly clear light. The light approaches swiftly, sweeps over the oaks and poplars like the headlights of a car – now I can already see a flying bird inside the trembling circle of light, the long, swanlike neck, the outspread wings, the handsome plumelike tail-feathers billowing out like a train. The Firebird plunges down behind the bushes and the whole garden lights up as if a thousand-kilowatt bulb had been switched on.

I leave my hiding-place and creep over to the raked

sandy patch where he dances, to see with my own eyes Tjudo tjudnoje Divo divnoje. At first it's hard to see anything at all – the light dazzles just like when you try to look at the sun. But gradually I get used to it and can make out the dancing bird in the swirl of sparks and streaks of light. I can see him tossing his head back, spreading his wings out and opening his wonderful tail like a fan. He is trembling from head to foot and his feathers flutter like flames in a breeze. Then he's gone again, and all I can see is a streak of fire and sparks like a dancing snake curling over the ground, finally ending in a swirling circle of fire.

Suddenly he stops and calls out to the birds all round the dance floor.

'Someone's watching! Someone unauthorized!'

'There's no unauthorized person here,' twitter the birds. 'The ladies have long since turned out the lamp. They're all asleep. We're quite alone.'

'No, someone's looking!' replies the Firebird. 'I can feel it all over me that someone's looking at me. Crane and Popotjka, go and see if someone's hiding behind the bushes.'

Crane and Popotjka walk round and look. After a while, Crane comes to the bush where I am hiding, sticks her head inside and sees me.

'There's someone here! More light please, Firebird, I can't see. Well now, if it isn't a little boy!'

'Come out!' calls the Firebird commandingly.

I get up and step trembling out on to the dance floor.

'I think I've seen you before,' says the Firebird, his voice coming from the crackling light in front of me.

'I'm sorry,' I stammer. 'I really didn't notice you. I thought . . . I thought there was nothing . . . otherwise I would never . . .'

'Oh well,' says the Firebird in more friendly tones, for he can see how ashamed I am. 'We'll say no more about it. But I must say I'm really annoyed with you for disturbing me like this over and over again. And yet I forgave you and gave you the chocolate egg.'

'How do you want us to punish him?' cries Popotjka. 'Shall we peck his eyes out? Because he was insolent enough to creep in here to watch your dance?'

'Let him be,' says the Firebird, raising his wing commandingly. 'He looks sad and unhappy. Tell me, little boy, what are you doing here in the rose garden in the middle of the night? Why aren't you at home asleep in bed like other children? Have you run away from home?'

'Yes,' I say, and I can feel the tears coming. 'I've run away and I'm never going back home again.'

'I thought as much!' cries Popotjka maliciously. 'And you know, when he was disobedient and fell in the lake . . .'

'Be quiet, Popotjka,' says the Firebird. 'I didn't ask you. Let him speak for himself and explain everything. Why don't you want to go back home?'

His voice is serious and sad, as if he already understands everything and is grieving with me over my misfortune.

I can't resist it any longer. I fall to my knees and burst into tears. 'Because . . .' I sob, '. . . because no one likes me. I want to be good and like everyone. But no one bothers about me. Everyone agrees with my enemy. No one wants to help me and protect me from him.'

'Who is your enemy?' says the Firebird gravely. 'And what has he done to you?'

'It's Kuno Grim. He makes my life unbearable. He has insulted and humiliated me, so I can never again show myself among people. Oh, help me, Firebird, help me take revenge, help me destroy him so that I can live!'

'Get up,' says the Firebird. 'Tell me what happened and I shall see if I can help you.'

I get up and tell him all about Kuno Grim. Once I've got going, I go on listing all my misfortunes and all the insults and injustices that have been inflicted on me. I tell the Firebird everything, not even leaving out Popotjka's nastiness: the way he teases me and offends me, and how it hurt when he nipped my finger. It is so simple and easy to talk about everything to him; he understands everything, although he says nothing and just listens.

'You poor boy,' he says at last. 'No one has suffered as you have. But do not grieve. I shall now put an end to your suffering, I promise you.'

I want to thank him, but he interrupts me.

'Enough said about these miseries. Come with me, boy. I like you. We shall dance together.'

I stand quite still, afraid of the firelight glowing in front of me. The birds also stand still in a semicircle, staring at me, only their shadows fluttering and wriggling in the sand and sliding gigantically enlarged over the rose-bushes round the edge.

'Didn't you hear what I said?' says the Firebird. 'I wish to dance with him. Rub some of the magic juice into him so that he doesn't burn up.'

We dance with each other all night, the birds watching in a circle round us.

'You know what,' whispers the Firebird, as we whirl round in the shower of sparks. 'I like you better than Crane and Popotjka. I like you best of all.'

The grasshoppers are playing quietly and apparently far away, a shower of shiny golden stars falling out of the darkness. I am so happy I don't even notice how the time is flying. The next moment, the night is over.

When I look up, the sky is light and as transparent as glass, the garden spreading out all around us, the leaves gleaming moistly green as if newly washed, and the roses no longer black but brilliant red. It is chilly and the light round the Firebird takes on a duller and duller golden red colour, as a lamp does when you've forgotten to turn it out in the morning.

'I must leave you now,' he says. 'But don't be afraid. I shall help you take a terrible revenge for all the injustices you have suffered. Never again will anyone be nasty to you or insult you.' He swings his lovely swan-neck back and pulls a feather out of his body. 'Hide this well and don't show it to anyone. When you hold it in your hand, you are the most powerful magician in the world.'

He hands me the soft, plumelike feather. It flutters and bends like a flame. A pale flamingo-pink light trembles in my hands, my arms and chest. Carefully, I fold the feather and hide it in my trouser pocket.

'The sun is coming up. I must go!'

The Firebird says goodbye to Crane and Popotjka and all the other birds crowd round him. Then he steps up to me, opens out his wings and presses me to his breast. The next moment he has gone and I can hear nothing but the rustle of his wing-feathers above my head and I see him disappearing high up above the tree-tops like a glittering comet.

The sun is flaring in Salmela's windows as if they were liquid copper and the white walls glow pink.

Whistling quietly, I walk up towards the house, the dew glittering on the rose leaves and the cobwebs slung between the hedges. I keep my hand in my trouser pocket and feel the glow of the magic feather on my fingertips. I dawdle on purpose, letting the toes of my shoes drag in the sand and stopping now and again to look at a bumble-bee or a honey-bee burying itself in an open rose. Sometimes I take a few dance steps in order to enjoy even more the intoxicating sense of power filling me.

The steps.

They are already sitting up there on the veranda having their morning tea. It is still early. The sky turns a transparent forget-me-not blue and the sun glows golden above the tree-tops. My shadow rises like a giant on the white wall. They still haven't seen me and have no idea I am so close.

The Grund aunts, Mamma and Bernt, they are all there. So is Kuno Grim, sitting beside Oliver, stirring his steaming glass of tea with a spoon. There are also a whole lot of strange uncles and aunts sitting around the festive table, smoking and talking and drinking tea, as if celebrating some happy event.

My heart is thumping, my knees shaking and I can't feel the steps under my feet as I go up them. But I am not afraid. On purpose and to annoy them, I maintain as casual a pose as I can, flinging my arms about and dragging my feet.

There is a deathly silence when they see me. Although I try not to, I can feel myself smiling as I step up to the table.

In the end, Mamma breaks the silence.

'Where have you been? We looked for you all last night. How dare you run away like that?'

'What's that got to do with you?' I say calmly.

A rustle of horror follows my insolent reply.

'Take him up to my room,' says Aunt Louise. 'He can stay there until he has thought better of it and apologized to his mother.'

'Ha ha,' I say. 'I'm not going anywhere.'

'I'll teach you,' exclaims Mamma, reaching out to tug at my hair.

A golden red wisp of flame. A pink ghostly light, sliding over the faces of those present and gone before anyone could blink. No one saw what I had in my hand.

'Anni!' screeches Aunt Louise, dropping the cup she had been holding under the samovar. 'Anni, let go!'

The others leap up and try to pull Mamma's hand away, which nevertheless has bored its way into Aunt Louise's shell-like coiffure right up to the knuckles and only reluctantly lets go. Mamma can't make out what's happening, rubs her eyes and looks round as if she has just woken up from a dream.

'Anni!' shrieks Aunt Louise, her whole body shaking and making the tea-service clatter and jump about on the table. She tries to tidy the streaky grey strands of hair hanging down over her forehead and put back the hairpins that have fallen on the table.

'What a way to behave! I'll certainly tell Muscha about this!'

'Just you wait until I get hold of you,' yells Bernt

vehemently. 'Shaming Mamma like that! What sort of trick is that?'

Another flash of lightning, perhaps even more dazzling than the previous one. The sunlight darkens and Bernt is struggling there in his chair in a blue-checked baby romper and with a messy bib round his neck, his fluffy head hardly above the table. He is drooling, his fingers in his mouth and chocolate cream and dribble running out of the corners of it.

'I'm hungry,' I say. 'Move over so I can sit down!'

'Now this has gone too far. He's not even been invited. Must we put up with such insolence?' a whole lot of indignant voices all cry at once.

I catch sight of Aunt Paula, who is eagerly whispering something to Uncle Bori. How odd that I hadn't noticed their faces just now! Uncle Bori pushes his plate away with a determined look and starts getting up from the table.

The next moment he is standing there dressed in Nina's pale-blue dress with a tuft of hair sticking out of the neckline and desperately trying to pull the skirt down over his hairy thighs. Aunt Paula has wet herself. You can hear it dripping and splashing under her chair. Her face is as red as a peony, her head on one side, and with her eyebrows raised and her smile stony she is staring at the slice of cake she is pretending to be interested in, turning it over with her fingertips.

'He scheems not to have had enough punischment,' says Kuno Grim, blowing a blue stream of smoke out of his mouth. 'He ought to have a really goot thraschsching. Come over here, my little friend.'

I go straight up to him. He jerks his head back in terror and presses his back against the basket chair as the lightning strikes. Now he's no bigger than a little boy of about four or five. He's wearing short blue trousers and a white blouse, just like me, though he still has his dark glasses and black beard. His whole body is shaking when I grab him by the collar and fling him across my knee.

'What do you say to this – and this?' I cry, the blows raining down on his little backside, the blue trousers stretched tightly across it. 'And this!'

I hit him so hard, my hand hurts after every blow. But the pain and the burning feeling only increase my rage and the intoxicating sense of power glowing within me. Kuno Grim's howls become shriller and shriller and with shorter and shorter gaps in between. He whimpers and weeps and begs me to stop. But I go on beating him.

'Don't kill him,' they cry all round me. 'He is a professor and he has sciatica. He's already had as much as he deserves.'

'Oh well,' I say finally, when my hand has become quite numb and has no feeling at all in it. 'Go down on your knees and beg for forgiveness. Oliver will come and sit beside me and from now on you'll leave the butterflies alone. Do you understand?'

'Enough, enough!' pleads Aunt Louise as Kuno Grim crawls up into his chair and covers his face with his handkerchief. 'Please, no more tricks. We'll do whatever you like. This is quite terrible.'

I sit down at the end of the table on a chair someone hastily pushes under me.

'Put the cake-dish in front of me,' I say. 'And give me some tea. I'm thirsty. No, none of that watery stuff, but real tea, like the grown-ups have. And ten – no, fifty lumps of sugar in it.'

'He's eating up everything,' they whisper all round me. 'Just think that he can get all that down. That huge fruit cake and now there's not a crumb left on the dish.'

'I'm still hungry,' I say. 'I want more food. I want ham and roast chicken and pike with egg sauce. Then I want grapes and pineapple, cream cakes and ice-cream – but it must be a mountain of ice-cream with strawberries on top. Fetch chocolates, lemonade and wine! I want to drink wine now I'm grown up. I intend to eat and drink everything there is in the world and as much as I like.'

'Heavens!' screeches Aunt Louise, clutching her

head in her hands. 'How can we get all that food here? He'll eat us out of house and home.'

'What schall we do?' says Kuno Grim. Now that he's stopped crying, at first he seems taken down a peg or two, but then he sits quietly for a long while, a thoughtful, worried crease in his forehead, his dark glasses directed unflinchingly at me. I think that's unpleasant and feel the heavy, penetrating gaze resting on my face as I eat and drink. 'Let him have what he wantsch.' Kuno Grim shrugs his shoulders lightly. 'It'sch good to schee hisch good appetite.'

'Go into the kitchen, Malla,' says Aunt Louise. 'See what we've got. Ask the maids to help with the cooking. Donna can't manage all that on her own. Or . . . wait, I'll go and look in the larder myself.'

Soon one steaming dish after another is carried in and placed in front of me. Everything a human being could wish for in the way of food piles up in front of me in glittering bowls, shiny tureens and gleaming dishes.

'I'm not mean,' I say. 'Although I have the right to eat up everything on my own, I have no wish to let you sit there looking on so hungrily. Tell me what you would like. This is to be a real feast. No, I'll serve you all myself. Don't look at the whipped cream so greedily, Aunt Paula. That's bad manners. And don't empty the sugar-bowl, Aunt Louise – a teaspoonful is more than enough in these hard times. Everyone is to have what they want except Kuno Grim, who shall have nothing. What would you like, Oliver? A little ice-cream or pineapple? No? Well, choose for yourself. Maybe you'd like a marzipan cake? That's the best of the lot, and I'll give it to you.'

Oliver's eyes shine and he smiles gratefully as I hand him the plate. Now that they all see I am being more friendly, they're no longer afraid, and they start laughing cheerfully and talking. Only the uncles and aunts I don't know appear to be amazingly indifferent and eat in silence. Kuno Grim sits sucking on his cigar, staring at me all the time.

I lift the lid off a casserole to help myself to chicken, but suddenly I see it's not chicken but a bluish-black crow, almost dried up to a skeleton with ants crawling all over it. I hurriedly put the lid back on, almost stunned by the stench. I lift the lid off the next casserole. It's not pork chops but roast bats. I rub my eyes and look again, but it's still roast bats. A spell has been put on everything. Instead of potatoes I see horse-dung, the peas are dead spiders, the soup is made of hair and feathers, and something so dark and slimy and vile is wriggling in the fish casserole I shudder all over when I glance under the lid.

Cautiously, I raise my eyes and look around. Heavens! Everywhere, on all the plates, there are piles of muck, waste and carrion, green blowflies buzzing round the table and the same nauseating, heavy stench as when we were approaching Kuno Grim's villa. But the others don't notice anything. Uncle Bori is contentedly sucking a mouldy rib-bone, Aunt Malla is trying to cut a piece off a dead mole lying on her plate. And Mamma is putting a fine, poisonous toadstool into her mouth and, smiling, says to Aunt Gulla: 'What delicious cream cakes. They must be from Stude's the confectioner's.'

'Stop!' I shriek. 'Throw it all away. Can't you see?' I jerk the feather out of my pocket and hold it up like a lamp.

Now they see it. Aunt Paula clears her throat and spits out the rotting corpse fat she had thought was ice-cream. Her eyes are popping and she almost vomits.

'But this is blood!' shrieks Aunt Louise. 'No wonder I thought there was something wrong with the red wine.'

'It wasn't me,' I cry as loudly as I can to drown the wails, curses and belches. 'Listen to me! It isn't my fault. It was someone else's spell. . . .'

I am interrupted by another scream, more awful and shriller than the others. I see Oliver stagger and fall with a dull thud to the floor by my chair. I have difficulty reaching him for all the horrified people rushing over and getting in my way. But Oliver is already dead. He is lying there with his eyes closed and his blue lips slightly apart. His head dangles loosely like a snapped-off flower when someone thrusts a hand under his back to lift him up. The marzipan cake I had selected for him was a snake's egg and he still has the shell in his hand.

'Out of the way!' shouts Uncle Bori, stamping on something awful that wriggles about under his heel. 'Don't come anywhere near. Ugh! Damned snake!'

'One moment,' says Kuno Grim, raising his hand. 'We've no time to losche. There'sch the murderer!' he stretches out his hand and points at me. 'He'sch the one who'sch schent the marschipan cake. Catsch him!'

I hear a menacing murmur behind me. The stranger uncles and aunts all repeat in chorus: 'Catch the murderer. He deserves to be killed.'

I don't bother to answer. Smiling, I lower the feather and touch Oliver's pale forehead. The others step aside and look on in silence. The feather flares up and strews a shower of stars over his face. They stick in his hair, fall on to his eyelids and go out.

The next moment Oliver leaps up and prances like a Red Indian all round the table. 'I'm alive again,' he exclaims. 'Ha, I'm pleased. Ha, I'm pleased.' He leaps over to me and presses me to him. Everyone round us is jubilant.

'So it wasn't you casting a spell on us. How can we possibly thank you for what you've done?'

I am close to tears but there is no time to lose. The moment for revenge and redress has come. 'No,' I say. 'It wasn't me. The person casting the spells is sitting here among you and I know who it is. I'll forgive you others.' I swing the feather. 'Everything will be as before, and I shall never cast any evil spells on you as long as you're kind to me. But him. . . .' I hold the feather out towards Kuno Grim, who starts and raises his hands to his glasses. 'He's my enemy. The enemy I'll never forgive.

'The moment for revenge has come,' I go on in a loud

voice. 'You like him. You sit at table with him. You spoil him with cream buns and cakes. Every day he sits here chatting and smoking, and you respectfully listen to everything he says. Just now you asked me to forgive him and I did as you wished. But you don't even know who he is. I presume you think he is . . .

'Look!' I say, going round the table, swinging the feather in front of all the stranger uncles and aunts. 'Look what he has brought with him and what you let into your house! Look at what you have been sitting at table with.'

The spell is broken. No longer are they well-dressed ladies and gentlemen sitting round the table, but Kuno Grim's wolfhounds and silver foxes, all sitting stiffly upright, their black paws on the table-cloth, their teeth bared in rigid grins.

'Bosje moi!' shrieks Aunt Louise. 'What company! What monsters! And we've been sitting at table with them. I have invited them to dinner. I took these people to be respectable, cultivated people you could mix with because I trusted Kuno and wished to be hospitable to his friends.'

'Don't you see who he is?' I cry, going up to Kuno Grim. 'Don't you know what it is like where he lives? Don't you know anything about the butterflies he spears on pins and keeps imprisoned in glass boxes? Didn't you notice he was the one to cast a spell on the food just now and let the snake bite Oliver? But I shall show you who he is.'

I go right up close to him. He is sitting absolutely still, his hands clamped on the arms of his chair, and he is staring straight at me as if he were just about to leap up.

'Do you think you can do anything to the mightiest magician in the world?'

I draw a huge ring of fire in the air with the feather and the monsters flee howling and wailing off the veranda.

'Look!' I shout, jerking off Kuno Grim's glasses, tearing off his cravat and starched collar and ripping his shirt open. He is still sitting without moving, like a dead man, glaring with the whites of his eyes. I put my fingers in his mouth. I pull out a pair of rattling jaws packed with shining crocodile teeth and fling them down on the floor.

'Ooooh!' they all cry. 'A magician.'

His hair and beard loosen when I pull at them and a bald, bluish-grey head is revealed. In front of us sits an apelike old man, the skin on his naked, wrinkled face almost black and his neck and chest covered with blue-black, feathery hairs.

Dead silence falls all round me.

Finally, Aunt Louise can be heard whispering: 'Bill, is it you?'

'Yes,' replies the horrible old man, smiling and getting up out of his basket chair. He rubs his hands together as if washing them, bows to right and left and rolls his eyes. Then he brays unctuously: 'Dear friends, dear brothers and sisters in Spirit, as we are now gathered together before . . .'

'Don't come near us!' screams Aunt Gulla. 'We were all at your funeral. What will Luscha say?'

But the vision lasts for only a few seconds. The feather! Now it's Kuno Grim – no, it's that horrible priest. It's not the horrible priest, it's Kuno Grim. It's something resembling them both. I hold out the feather. It's a scarecrow that falls to pieces. It's a gigantic toad lolloping across the floor. It has Kuno Grim's beard and glasses. I stamp on it. It seems almost squashed flat and half dead. It still doesn't want to die, although its head is squashed flat so that it no longer has a face. One foreleg is still wriggling. I take it by its long white toes, go round the corner of the house and fling it on to the gravel by the kitchen steps.

I see the blind dogs biting it. After a while it is nothing but a shapeless lump covered with grains of sand and flies.

We're having a marvellous party. I conjure up everything beautiful and wonderful in the world. The table is groaning with delicacies and flowers, giant blue and yellow balloons swaying ponderously up in the ceiling and glittering streamers spinning us all into a red, green and white network.

'Now let's have some fun,' I say to Oliver. 'Do you want to see how high I can jump?'

I take off and bounce like a ball over Aunt Louise's head across the table. Another leap – everyone screams – the veranda railing flashes beneath me – I'm down in the garden and flying upwards again, rising in a steep curve over the tree-tops. My stomach feels hollow and my mouth turns dry as I look down and land on the red roof of Salmela. How small the flower-beds and rose hedges look from up here, like the pattern on a colourful cloth. The others are standing down there like dolls, pointing at me. The next leap takes me so giddily high up into blue space I can no longer distinguish them. I brush by a downy cloud and see the sun golden yellow and fearful flashing above me. Right down there I can just see the roof of Salmela and the trees in the park as if at the bottom of a well.

'Well, can I jump then?' I pant, as once again I join the others by the veranda railing.

'You were so high up, we couldn't see you at all,' says Oliver, looking at me with fascination. 'I thought you'd stay up there for ever.'

'Do you want to see how strong I am?'

I seize Aunt Louise and throw her up into the air. Her skirt unfolds like an umbrella and twirls round. She shrieks and gropes about in the air with her hands. I take her and throw her up to the tree-tops again.

'You mustn't!' she screams. 'Stop it. Help! Help! He's killing me.'

'It's all right, I meant you no harm,' I say, and put her down. But she falls over and lies with her legs in the air. 'I can show you in another way.'

I push my hand in under the stone base of the house and slowly lift it up with all its towers and pinnacles and protruding balconies. It is a little difficult to balance the whole building on the palm of my hand and it sways and creaks like a ship at sea. Dishes and glasses slide about on the table and clatter into each other. Aunt Gulla has stayed on the veranda and is clinging screaming on to the railing.

'Put the house down again, for God's sake,' they all cry. 'Don't take away our home. Supposing you drop it?'

'Well, I'm strong, aren't I?' I say to Oliver, smiling at him. 'Not even Uncle Bori can lift such a large house.'

'Shouldn't we go inside again now the house is back in place?' says Aunt Louise. 'I think it's slightly chilly out here.'

I take Oliver by the hand and we hurry into the salon, where pearly ribbons of bright lanterns are hanging in the palms and myrtle-bushes. We go over to a large dark mirror.

The little boy standing beside Oliver looks like a prince. He is wearing a black velvet jacket, breeches and a yellow silk shirt, a silver plume in his hat. When he moves in the mirror, you could take him for a butterfly. I have never seen such a beautiful boy in all my life. He's even more beautiful than Oliver. 'Look,' I say, turning round. 'Look at me.'

Oliver puts his hand on my shoulder, looking gravely and thoughtfully at me without answering. Then suddenly he smiles. 'Do you want to be my friend?' he says.

'Yes,' I whisper. 'Your best and only friend. You'll always like me best and play with me and never leave me. And you'll always take me in your arms whenever I want.'

Oliver laughs and pulls me up on his knee. I clap my hands and cry out: 'Now everything's all right. Now I want you all to be happy and have more fun than you've ever had in your lives before. Everyone is to dance and sing and laugh and eat and never go to bed. And the fun will never come to and end.

'But where is Nina?' I say when I see the dancers

pouring into the salon. 'I want her to be here so that I can dance with her. I want her to be here, and Kotik and Borja and Aljoscha as well. So she sees I'm the best-looking, the strongest and most agile boy in the world.'

But I've hardly had time to utter this wish, when Oliver puts me down. I hear the sound of heavy footsteps and when I look up Kuno Grim is standing in the middle of the salon floor looking at me in silence, as if waiting for me to leave.

'Out!' I shout furiously. 'You've no business here. You're dead. You don't exist at all.'

'I've never been scho alive asch I am now,' says Kuno Grim with an evil smile, twirling his dark beard.

'You won't deceive me a second time!' I yell. 'This is the end of all your tricks.'

I put my hand in my pocket, but it's empty. Have I dropped the feather? When I turn round, Oliver has gone too.

'Just you wait until I've got hold of my magic feather,' I cry and rush towards the door.

'Magic feather!' Kuno Grim bursts out laughing. 'Vot are you talking about? Magic feather? You nevver had one.'

'The Firebird's feather,' I cry. 'Which made me into the mightiest magician in the world. I should think you've already had enough of its powers. Just you watch out.'

'But the Firebird haschn't given you any feather at all. All that hasch never happened.'

'How could it never have happened?' I exclaim. 'I've . . .'

'It wasch to happen firscht tonight and tomorrow. But it'll never happen because you've juscht made it all up.' Kuno Grim pulls out his big gold watch and looks at it. 'It'sch a long time till it'sch dark. You've been hidden under the busches by the schtone wall all the time and it'sch only a few hoursch ago I gave you a good schpanking.'

Anguished, I look around, but the walls wobble, the room spins round, everything dissolves and even Kuno Grim himself melts away as if in a mist. 'You'd better go off to wherever you really were all the time,' he says.

The last thing I see is the pocket-watch Kuno Grim is holding under my nose – its face with its mysterious symbols, the thin gold hands that stick out in different directions and look like a mother and a father and a baby trotting round all the time.

30

I WAS SITTING IN THE LILAC-BUSHES AGAIN, RAINDROPS plopping on the leaves. The teaspoon and Nina's ragged doll's blanket were still there, and the ants were rushing to and fro as before in the sand in front of my knees.

Nothing of what I had just gone through was true. Kuno Grim was the more powerful of the two of us, and as if to show his power properly and humiliate me even more, he now appeared down there in the rose garden together with Oliver. Through the network of branches I saw them appear and then become hidden by the hedges and quickly vanish in the direction of the aunts' house.

I was really rather bored sitting there. Why did no one come? Why didn't anyone notice I had gone? What could the time be? Had Mamma and Bernt completely forgotten me and already gone home?

I crept out and looked up at the castle-like house. That's where my enemy was. His presence filled the whole house and made it so repugnant and hateful I felt I would never again be able to bring myself to go inside as long as he was there.

Cautiously I crept on along the stone wall, now and again crouching down so as not to be seen. Perhaps they were hiding behind the curtains in there, spying on me. The thought of Kuno Grim standing by the window watching me creeping about, perhaps beckoning to Oliver and mockingly pointing at me, infuriated me. I was just going to creep as close to the house as possible without being seen in order to look at it for the very last time, to find out what they were all doing at the moment. Then I would turn back, run away and leave them for ever.

The grass was wet and, when I pushed aside the branches, a shower of cold drops rattled down on my head and neck. Twigs and gravel stuck to my knees and it hurt when I pressed them to the ground.

Suddenly something bluish shone through an opening in the bushes. As I crept nearer, I saw a whole lot of feathers on the ground, bits of shiny gold down rising in the air when I breathed on them and large speckled feathers with strong quills and comblike webs that stuck together like fingers. Loveliest of all was a bunch of huge plumes, almost as long as myself. The quill was covered with thick golden hair that fluttered softly in the wind and at the top, the feathers broadened out into glowing deep-blue eyes, blazing like an angel's and surrounded by a wreath of golden rays.

I at once recognized them. They were the Firebird's feathers lying scattered in front of me. And although I saw they were very like peacock feathers and I knew the Firebird was golden red and not blue, that didn't matter. For the time when the Firebird showed himself up on the stone wall and frightened me with his scream, he had looked quite different and had perhaps resembled a peacock.

But something horrible had happened here. Some of the feathers were blood-stained and the grass was trampled, the broken stems covered with something black and sticky rather like tar. When I lifted the hand I was leaning on, a tiny blob of red trembled on the back of my hand like redcurrant jelly.

I heard someone calling and the sound of running footsteps in the garden. It was Oliver looking for me.

I was so shaken by the horrible discovery I'd made, I just ran straight to him. Panting and excited, he leant over to say something, but I got there before him. 'Come and see!' I cried, catching hold of his hand. 'You must come and see. Someone's hurt the Firebird.'

Oliver frowned when he saw the heap of feathers. 'It must have been one of the dogs or the silver foxes from up there. One of the foxes got out the night before last.'

'Do you think he's alive? Maybe he's managed to get away and is hiding somewhere so the fox can't find him. Let's go and look.'

Oliver bent down and poked about in the feathers. When he lifted up some matted wet quills stuck to each other, a number of dark, light-shy creepy-crawlies were revealed, and they scattered as quick as lightning and hid in the earth.

'He's probably dead,' said Oliver. 'But come now. Your mother and Bernt are waiting for you down by the jetty.' He picked up a big rainbow feather and handed it to me. 'Do you want to keep this? As a souvenir?'

A cold raw wind was blowing through the garden and rustling threateningly in the trees. The sun appeared now and again from behind grey veils of cloud but was pale and dull like a moon.

I noticed then that the rose garden looked different from before – shabbier and not so well cared for. The trees were old and tired, the lawn brown and uneven, and there were weeds everywhere in the flower-beds, hiding the flowers still out in them. There were no bees or butterflies in sight. The roses were dead, a green star with a wreath of scorched hair in the middle all that was left of them. Horrid pale-green spiders with egglike, swollen rear bodies were spinning their webs between the branches. We went past a hedge whose leaves were covered with dark spots and full of holes as if moth-eaten. Up in a weeping birch was a clump of yellowish golden leaves, and the sandy path was covered with dead petals.

The only thing still really lovely was the feather I had in my hand. It coiled itself round, sparkling and trembling as if alive. Sometimes I thought it opened and closed its wonderful eye. I was afraid it would tear itself out of my hand and fly away.

The Firebird was dead. He would never again come to the rose garden at night to dance his wonderful dance. In vain would the grasshoppers play in the foliage and the moon shed his silver light over the garden. From now on, the raked sandy patch would be deserted and empty, and the birds would crouch sorrowfully in a circle round the edge. In his secretive way, he had sustained the whole of this world of beauty, and now he no longer existed.

Aunt Louise and Aunt Malla had gone with Mamma right down to the jetty. When Aunt Malla heard what had happened, she took out her little handkerchief, pressed it to her eyes and sighed – wasn't that what she had always said? They should dismiss Kuno Grim and ask him to leave. They had had nothing but trouble since they had handed the garden over to him. But then Aunt Louise became dreadfully frightened, looked up at the house and waved her hands about.

'Sh, sh, sh! He can hear what you say. Not another word on the subject, Malla!'

When Oliver went over and kissed Mamma's hand, she said: 'So we shan't be seeing you again until next summer.'

Oliver grimaced. 'I'm leaving the day after tomorrow,' he said. 'School starts soon.' He lifted me up. 'Next summer you'll be so big and strong I shan't be able to hold you like this.'

I tickled his face with the feather and he closed his eyes and laughed. I wanted him to kiss me and held out my lips, but he didn't understand. When I realized he was about to put me down, I was afraid and clung on to him. He suddenly understood, pressed his lips to mine, then put me down. But everything had happened so quickly, I hardly had time to notice before it was over.

'Hurry, now,' cried Aunt Louise. 'It may rain any minute.'

Oliver pushed the boat out and we glided off across the bumpy, greyish-brown waves, the rushes swaying in the wind. Now and again a gust of wind came along, the water darkened and crinkled like snakeskin. Over on the shore the aunts were waving their handkerchiefs, and Oliver also raised his hand and waved to me. The wind was pulling and tugging at the aunts' clothing as if they were flying, and lifting Oliver's hair so that it fluttered like a Red Indian's.

'You don't usually kiss strangers on the mouth,' said Mamma, holding the oars still. 'You kiss your mother and father and grandmother and others who belong to the family – but not strangers.'

'Boys don't usually kiss each other,' cried Bernt from the stern. 'They don't like it at all. You behave like a baby.'

I could feel myself going red and looked away. 'They do like it,' I stammered. 'You don't know anything.'

'What's that you've got in your hand?' Mamma interrupted. 'Where did you get hold of that feather?'

When I told her, she told me to give it to her.

'Heavens! It's got blood on it.' She turned the feather in her hand, her mouth pursed. 'Something's crawling in it.'

'Now you've broken it!' I cried in horror, for Mamma was holding the feather so carelessly, the wind broke off the top where the rainbow eye was. 'It's the Fire-Peacock's feather.'

'You simply don't understand,' said Mamma. 'The peacock may have died of some terrible disease. And that fox or dog that bit it may have had rabies. It's full of bacteria.'

She flung the feather away and grasped the oars again.

The feather whirled away in the wind, then appeared again on the crest of a wave, glistening and glowing in all its colours like a patch of oil. We hurriedly moved on.

I crept sobbing up into the prow. Dear God, I thought, why have you given me a mamma like that? Why must I have a mamma like no other child's mother? Someone who thinks everything that's fun in the world is dangerous, and who forbids everything? It'd be better to have no mother at all.

31

MAMMA HAS DISAPPEARED. SHE IS NOWHERE TO BE FOUND – neither in Grandmother's room when we go in to say good-morning to Grandmother, nor in her own bedroom where her bed is. She isn't at the dinner-table or with the others when they are having their afternoon coffee. In the evening when Aunt puts us to bed, we wait in vain for Mamma to come in and talk to us and say good-night, and we can't hear her voice from the salon when the grown-ups sit round the lamp talking while we're trying to go to sleep.

Whenever I ask where Mamma is, they always say she has gone away, that she's in Viborg and living in a hospital with Dr Montelius and she can't come home for a while. And they look so peculiar and solemn, I don't like to ask more. At first it felt rather strange with Mamma suddenly becoming invisible and distant like that, just as if she no longer existed. But I have got used to it now, and find it quite natural that Mamma's always away. I don't believe Aunt and Grandmother when they say Mamma will soon be coming home again. Because she won't be coming, however often they say so, and I've just stopped asking. Mamma can't come home, because she doesn't exist in the same way as Grandmother and Aunt and the others you can see and hear and talk to. She exists only like a picture when you close your eyes, or you're absorbed in your thoughts, or she comes to you in a dream. She has become like God and the angels and the spirits and all the other secretive creatures living their own lives in some incomprehensible distant place and visiting you only when you're alone. And really it's much better that way. For although you're sometimes sad about her and would be glad if you suddenly heard her voice in the hall, it's good that Aunt now looks after all of us. She likes me best and I never need be annoyed by seeing Bernt on the sofa with Mamma when I'm taken off to bed, or seeing her kiss and hug Tommy. Actually, she has really always been a picture like that and has never existed in the proper way, although I haven't noticed it before.

One morning, Aunt comes in with that rye porridge we always complain about and says: 'I've got a secret – a very, very nice secret. If you're good boys and eat up without complaining, I'll tell you it.'

'Tell us,' we say, because Aunt is smiling contentedly and her face looks as if she really has found out something interesting and exciting. But Aunt tells us nothing until the bottoms of our plates are white and shiny and we've scraped off the horrid brown ring round the edges, then licked the spoon.

'Now I'll tell you,' she says. 'You've got a little brother. He was born last night.'

I am disappointed and disconcerted. Judging by Aunt's expression, you would have expected something much more fun and exciting.

'Can I go and see him?' I say.

'Don't be so idiotic,' says Bernt. 'You can't see him now. He's with Mamma in hospital.'

Of course it was silly of me not to think about that at once. When a child is born, it is at once in its mother's arms or in a cradle by her, and she kneels in front of it with clasped hands and is pleased, just as you see in the pictures of the infant Jesus.

'What does he look like?' says Bernt.

'He's awfully sweet. Pappa telephoned just now from town and said he's never seen such a sweet, clever baby. He weighs three kilos.'

It doesn't really make any difference how much he weighs or what Pappa thinks about him. As he isn't here, he can't possibly be real either, just as Mamma hasn't been real since she went away to hospital.

'Aren't you pleased?' says Aunt, bending down to kiss me. 'Just think, now you're already so big you've got two little brothers.'

I don't know whether I'm all that terribly pleased. One little brother is really more than enough. Recently he's got quite big so you can play with him and be with him, but why should I be pleased to have another, who is also even smaller and more trouble than the one I've already got?

'Was he born with his shirt on like Tommy?' I ask. 'Is he a Sunday's child?'

But Aunt says he can't be that because today is Wednesday. And he was born quite naked, just as Bernt and I were.

'Where did he come from?' I ask. 'Where do little children come from when they're born?'

'I've told you,' says Aunt. 'Many a time. The stork comes flying in with the little baby in its beak and lets it down into the basket by Mamma's bed.'

'Do you mean the stork came with our little brother last night while Mamma was asleep?'

'Yes, of course.'

'But how did he get in?'

'Someone must have left the window open, because we were expecting him, you see. Or perhaps the stork let him down the chimney, as storks often do.'

'But where did the stork get hold of the baby?'

'From the water-lily pool. You've seen the picture lots of times.'

'Show me again.'

Aunt takes the book off the shelf and turns over the pages.

It's a pool or a lake of deep-blue water like the channel beyond our boat jetty. White water-lilies and green water-lily leaves float on the water and there's a baby on every single leaf. There are even two babies on some of the leaves, with their arms round each other's necks. All of them have their eyes closed and know nothing at all about what's going on around them. But quite near a chubby baby with golden brown curls and pink toes a stork is already waiting with a napkin under its wing, stretching out his long red beak to lift up the baby and put the napkin on it. You can see another stork far away among the clouds, with its wings out and a white bundle in its beak. He's already picked up a baby from the pool and is on his way to the mamma.

'But where do the babies come from to the water-lily pool?' I ask.

'Don't ask so many questions,' says Aunt. 'They're just there, lying sweetly asleep until the stork fetches them.'

When Aunt has gone, I go on looking at the picture. It's amazing that I don't remember the water-lily pool or the stork with its lovely white feathers and red beak. Nor do I remember the other babies lying asleep all round me. Was I alone on my leaf, or did I have a friend beside me, as pink-fingered and chubby as myself? I must have been sleeping so soundly I couldn't feel anything. But I must have some kind of memory of the water-lily pool, because otherwise it wouldn't feel so nice and at the same time so sad to look at the picture. Perhaps it's the memory of a profound joy that I've never experienced since, but which has lasted for centuries while I was deep in a dreamless sleep. When I think really hard about it, I can just dimly remember the water round me, the ripple and splash of water, or perhaps just the soft, gliding movement of the water and the sleepy swaying as the water-lily leaf rose and fell beneath me. That was where the animals found me, and when the stork carried me to Mamma, they came too, looked after me and played with me until they left me for ever. The actual memory of that strange life has got less and less clear and soon the loss of it will be the only thing left. The loss of the water-lily pool, the deep sleep and those creatures who loved me in a different way from the way people do.

'How long do you think I slept in the water-lily pool before the stork came and fetched me?' I ask Bernt.

'There's no water-lily pool,' says Bernt, smiling in a superior way.

'Of course there is. Aunt said so.'

'All that about water-lily pools and storks is just nonsense. You were inside Mamma. It's the same with all babies.'

I look suspiciously at Bernt. He is looking self-important, as if he had said that just to annoy me.

'All babies are inside their mothers to start with. At first they're as tiny as a seed, but they grow all the time and, when they're big enough, they come out.'

'How do they come out?' I say distrustfully, for Bernt's story sounds so strange I can't believe it just like that.

'Through the bottom, of course. And when the baby has come out from the mother, they say he's been born.'

'But then it comes out just like bigs.' I laugh loudly – what Bernt has said sounds so funny.

'The mother's in a terrific hurry, but when she sits on the pot, a baby comes. And she's terribly surprised.'

We both burst out laughing.

'I expect it happens so quickly, it comes in her trousers or falls into the lavatory. . . .'

What Bernt is telling me is awfully funny and exciting because it's forbidden and naughty, and Aunt and Grandmother would be angry if they heard us. But when my eye falls on the picture of the water-lily pool again, I don't want to listen to Bernt any more. For the picture of the stork and the sleeping baby is so lovely, and I can feel that I've been there, that it's part of my past, my lost life, so it is true. What Bernt says is dirty and unpleasant, and although it made a good joke to laugh at, it was annoying in the long run to hear him talk such nonsense in that way.

'You're talking rubbish,' I say angrily. 'Of course I've been in the water-lily pool, and a stork flew high up among the clouds with me in his beak. I remember it myself.'

'There is no pool like that, and storks are only found in Germany and Denmark. They never come here.'

'Of course there are storks, though you've never seen them.'

'How could a stork get into a hospital, then? And what would happen to the babies on the water-lily leaves? They'd freeze to death, and when it was windy they'd fall into the water and drown.'

'You're lying!' I shout, more and more disturbed by Bernt's evidence. 'Aunt told me and she's grown up and knows better than you.'

'Aunt probably knows she's deceiving you. Only you and Tommy are stupid enough to believe what she says.'

'She's not deceiving us. It's you who's trying to deceive us.'

'Didn't you notice anything about Mamma before she went into hospital?'

'You're lying! You're lying!' I scream, for Bernt's manner is getting more and more annoying. 'I'll tell Grandmother about all the filthy things you said. All that about insides and bottoms and bigs . . .'

'Sneak!'

Bernt jumps up on to my bed and we start fighting.

He presses my face into the pillow so that I can't get any air. But then the door creaks and he lets me go. Grandmother is standing there, her face grave and unmoving, and she doesn't look at all pleased about the new baby. 'Aren't you ashamed of making such a noise?' she says, and her voice is so quiet and extraordinary, it frightens me. 'Go back to your bed at once, Bernt.'

'But is it true we've got a little brother, Grandmother?' cries Bernt.

'Yes,' says Grandmother, looking past us out of the window as if she'd seen something awful and unknown out there. 'But you should be ashamed of making such a noise. Mamma is very, very ill.'

Her voice is such that I daren't ask anything. She sees what's happening in Viborg, beyond the mountains and lakes. But we can't see what it is that's happening there, so we're frightened and daren't move.

Finally, when Grandmother has finished looking, she turns her tired eyes on us. 'What do you think God thinks if children just make a noise and laugh while their mother is ill and close to death?'

We don't know what to say, so say nothing.

'Sit up and clasp your hands,' says Grandmother. 'We must pray for Mamma, so that God doesn't think you are heartless and ungrateful children who don't even mind about keeping their mother.'

Grandmother sits down in the armchair, closes her eyes and waits for a moment. When it is quite quiet so that nothing stops God hearing every single word, Grandmother opens her eyes, lifts her head and starts talking to him. We say the words after her as best we can, but I daren't say them aloud because God would notice that sometimes I say things wrong and find it difficult to pronounce all those peculiar long words.

Grandmother thanks God for giving us a little brother. She says it is a great gift, that he has been merciful to us and listened to our prayers when we have asked him for a little brother (although we never have).

She says: 'Blessed art thou, Lord Zebaoth, Lord of the Heavens, Heaven is thy throne and the Earth thy footstool. Thou hast given life to this child and instilled the eternal divine spark in his soul.'

Then we beg God for forgiveness for being heartless and ungrateful and showing Mamma too little love and obedience. We pray that God shall not punish us for this by taking her away from us. That he will soon let her come back from the hospital. Then we promise always to be good and obedient children. Then Grandmother says: 'Have mercy, Lamb of God, thou who bears all the sins of the world on thy shoulders.'

When Grandmother sits there with her eyes on the ceiling, she sees right through the boards and beams into heaven, and she sees God and his Lamb sitting right on top of the clouds, listening to what we are saying. But we can't see through a ceiling. I'm rather glad we can't, actually, because otherwise I would be even more frightened and find it even more difficult to say the words after Grandmother. God probably looks very grim now as he looks down on us and listens. And it's not certain the Lamb standing beside him with a sackful of sins on his shoulders would be able to persuade him. Somewhere, far away in hospital, are Mamma and that little brother who has never existed before and now suddenly does. Something awful has happened to Mamma, and it's our fault, because God is angry with us. But he's not only annoyed with us for making a noise and fighting like that when he has given us a little brother. He was really angry when he heard all that we said about babies, because of course he heard every word, although perhaps Grandmother didn't.

32

SINCE THAT LITTLE BROTHER WAS BORN OVER THERE IN THE hospital, everything has been dull and awful. When you walk through a room, it's as if something invisible were lying in wait behind the chairs, behind the sofas, behind the closed doors or inside the dark cupboards. When something creaks behind you, a door or the sound of footsteps in the next room, you start and turn round with your heart thumping. But everything is quite still and all the things are looking gravely and sternly at you, as if they disapproved of you for so openly showing you're afraid.

Sometimes even the things can't help showing their terror. They start trembling and shaking – only slightly, of course, so you don't notice it at first. But when you've seen it and you go from room to room, you notice that all the things are shaking with fright. The little porcelain figures above the dining-room sofa tinkle and wobble hither and thither, and the water in the carafe slops. The black wooden elephant on the smoking table clatters on its big, flat feet and the whole house seems to be shaking with fear, but then it calms down again and everything is quiet and still.

The grown-ups' faces are serious and closed. They don't smile at you as before, and they don't seem to like you any more. Their voices have become harsh and impatient. They're always in a hurry, aunts and uncles coming and going. Pappa appears and disappears again. Uncle Georg shuts himself up with Grandmother in her room. Suddenly there's an awful lot of telephoning, about Mamma and about the hospital. Sometimes they talk in loud and excited voices. Aunt blows her nose and wipes her eyes with her handkerchief. When the grown-ups notice you're in the room, they don't like it and push you into another room. They close the doors so that you won't hear what they're saying. Sometimes they all sit around saying nothing, someone occasionally clearing his throat and saying a word or two in such a low voice anyone or anything nearby can't hear it. Then they all sit saying nothing again.

You're never allowed to be really happy, to play or make a noise, or laugh as before. As soon as you have forgotten all that misery and start laughing and shouting and rushing through the rooms, Grandmother is sad. Aunt comes and scolds you and chases you into the nursery. It seems like Good Friday all the time. On Good Friday you also have to be quiet and still and never laugh, but just think about miserable things. For Grandmother says it's a sin to be happy when Jesus is hanging on the cross waiting for death. You have to keep thinking about how the nails hurt his hands and feet, and how the crown of thorns lacerates his forehead. Now we have to think about Mamma being ill all the time. We must never forget it, and have to go on being quiet and miserable.

Every evening when Grandmother says prayers with us, we pray to God that he will make Mamma well again. But she just gets worse and worse, and even more awful and incomprehensible things happen over there in Viborg. It's very difficult to understand all that, because the grown-ups don't want us to know anything and send us out of the room as soon as there's talk about Mamma. But anyhow I do understand from the few words I have managed to catch that it is all a terrible secret.

When Grandmother went out into the hall with Aunt Luscha, she said: 'She doesn't get enough air. She keeps saying she's suffocating and demands that they open all the windows.'

There's a creature who's even more dangerous than the Devil, Satan and Beelzebub, and whom I fear more than all the ghosts, spooks and monsters who collect round our house at night. That's Death. He lives over in the churchyard, where Grandfather and Great-Grandfather,

Great-Grandmother Gromley, old Uncle Bill and many other ancient aunts and uncles are buried.

Now Death has settled on Mamma. He has flown off to the hospital and is sitting on her, weighing her chest down as if she had a great mountain on top of her. She doesn't get enough air and shouts that the windows must be opened so she can breathe in some of the cool, fresh breezes out there. But Death won't let her breathe. He's trying to strangle Mamma and is squeezing her throat with his skeletal fingers. No one can get him off Mamma and help her as she struggles with him. Day and night he sits crouched on her bed without letting go of her throat. He's waiting for her strength to give out so that he can take her with him.

That's what Death is like. He is envious of everything living and beautiful, and just likes destroying and annihilating, so that in the end nothing is left. No one is allowed to be happy and have fun for more than a short while. Then your time is past, the fun is over for ever and you can expect nothing but eternal darkness. Death kills butterflies and grasshoppers, lets flowers wither and trees rot, and even decomposes stones. In due time, he comes to everyone. No one can escape him, and it doesn't matter whether you live for a day only like a butterfly or you have three hundred years to live like the tortoise – in the end he is there all the same and puts an end to the joy. I have seen several pictures of him in which he is leading old men and women to the grave. But sometimes they are kings and knights with sweeping plumes in their hats and ladies in lovely billowing dresses. They don't trot along quite meekly beside Death, with sorrowful, downcast eyes like the old men and women, but turn away and shriek and resist. But Death doesn't let go of their hands, he goes inexorably on with them. Sometimes Death also comes to a mother sitting rocking her baby, snatches the baby out of her arms and runs away with it.

As Death just goes on and on sitting on Mamma,

never letting her go, Grandmother finally gets impatient. Maybe the prayers we say with her every evening don't help, because despite everything she tells us not to do, we aren't always as quiet and sorrowful as God wants us to be. Our disobedience and the trouble we cause make Death over there in the hospital so strong and heavy, no one can have any effect on him. And God doesn't help us, because I so often forget to think about Mamma and what a bad time she is having.

One morning, Uncle Georg comes into the living-room in a dripping oilskin and with raindrops in his beard. 'They've just phoned from the hospital, Muscha,' he says. 'It's serious.'

'Take the children out!' Grandmother says to Aunt, looking sternly at us.

'I've told Ali to harness the horses,' adds Uncle Georg, but after that I don't hear any more, because Aunt takes us into the nursery and closes the door.

When Uncle Georg has gone and we are allowed out of the nursery, Grandmother is getting dressed to go away. Njanjan is helping her put on a black cloak. Kirsti the kitchen-maid is standing there with the umbrella in her hand and Aunt is on her knees in front of Grandmother, fastening the buckles on her overshoes.

'Goodbye,' says Grandmother, running her hand over our heads. 'I must go and see Mamma. Be good and obedient and pray for her this evening.'

I should like to ask Grandmother why she is going away and what she is going to do at the hospital. But her face is so stern and serious I dare not. It's bound to be something awful, that Mamma's strength is giving out and that Death is perhaps suffocating her. The grown-ups look so miserable and Aunt's face is quite red and glistening. She keeps it hidden as she bends over, busy with Grandmother's overshoes. But perhaps it's all a good thing, because now Grandmother's patience has given out and she herself has decided to go to Viborg to drive away Death. Then it could happen that Death will be afraid.

Then we all stand by the window, looking at the carriage standing by the kitchen steps. It's the finest carriage of all, with beautifully curved and lacquered mudguards, lamps and red spokes, and a black hood like a mussel. Uncle Georg is in the driving seat. The horses are stamping impatiently with their hoofs and champing on their bits. Grandmother leans forward under the hood to take the cases and umbrella with the tortoise-shell handle and all the rest of the things Njanjan and Aunt hand up to her. Uncle Georg cracks the whip, the horses toss their heads and the red spokes start turning. Suddenly there is a crack like a shot, sparks fly from the horses' hoofs and a blue flash of lightning flares under the wheels. The whole carriage takes a little leap up into the air and the next moment it has gone.

I can't go to sleep that night. I keep seeing the room with the white bed where Mamma is lying with Death sitting astride her chest in his black hood. Grandmother is in the middle of the room calling to Death to go away and pointing at the door with the sharp end of her umbrella. But Death refuses to go, and keeps turning his black holes of eyes and his worn-away nose on Grandmother, showing his teeth like a dog with a bone. The windows are open, the white curtains fluttering, and the night outside is silent and dark and boundless.

Mamma cries out: 'Help! Help! Why don't you open the windows? I'm suffocating! I'm suffocating!'

Death leans forward and squeezes his hands round Mamma's throat so that his fingers cut into it like a noose. Then Grandmother strikes his hands with her umbrella so hard, he has to let go. She hits him on the head, on his back and shoulders. She takes him by the armpits, by the shoulders and by the waist from behind, and tries to lift him so she can drag him off the bed. But Death makes himself as heavy as he can and clings on to the mattress with his fingers and toes. Grandmother can lift him only a little, because he's as heavy as lead – then, panting heavily, she has to put him down again.

In the end, Grandmother starts wrestling with Death. She wrestles with him on Mamma's bed. Death seizes hold of her hair and snaps at her hands with his jaws. Sometimes Grandmother manages to throw him off the bed and they wrestle on the floor, Grandmother pushing Death towards the door. But then he wins again and is suddenly back sitting up on Mamma's bed. But Grandmother is tough. She has wrestled with God for a whole night and almost been victorious, so why should she give up this time? Grandmother and Death go on struggling with each other like this, but I can't keep up with them any longer and finally fall asleep, away from it all.

In the morning, when I wake up, the sun is shining now and again through the clouds. It has stopped raining, though the raindrops glitter in the spruce branches and Aunt's face is friendly and safe when she says: 'Grandmother phoned from town just now to say Mamma is much better today. The doctor has said she'll probably be well again soon.'

Now I know that Grandmother has won the battle and has driven Death off Mamma's bed. Mamma can breathe again now, her temperature has gone down and we needn't be afraid she will die. We can play again, and no one stops us making a noise. When Uncle Georg comes to talk to Aunt that day, we aren't sent out but are allowed to hear him telling Aunt that Mamma has already asked for a little bouillon and said it was good, and that she sent her love to us all and asked us to be good and obedient until she comes home. In the evening, when we're saying our prayers with Aunt, we thank God for listening to us and saving Mamma, so that we don't have to be poor little motherless beggar-children. But I think it's actually rather unfair to give God all the credit in this matter. It's not *him* but Grandmother who has dispersed Death's darkness and given new life to Mamma. God just sat there looking on, cogitating and dawdling about, not bothering to help at all, although we kept asking him to evening after evening.

Grandmother stays away for a few more days, because she has to sit on guard by Mamma's bed. It could happen that Death would come back and try again to take Mamma from us. But he keeps out of the way now – he clearly doesn't dare take up the struggle again. Mamma is getting better and better all the time.

One day the grand carriage with lamps and red spokes stops again outside our door. Pappa jumps down from the driving seat and Grandmother leans forward under the hood. Inside beside her is something strange and awful in a black hood and with a white cloth over its face.

Grandmother hands a number of cases and parcels out to Aunt and Njanjan and the others standing below. At first so many rugs and shawls and cushions come that Aunt's arms can hardly handle them and the fringes drag in the gravel. Then comes a large basket with wrinkly lace round the edge and something pale blue and fluffy inside it. And, finally, Grandmother very carefully hands out a large grey bundle of clothing to Njanjan, who takes it just as carefully. She doesn't put it down among the other things on the ground, but holds it in her arms and looks at it and laughs and pouts her lips as if she meant to kiss it.

Then they go over to the steps, Njanjan first with the grey bundle in her arms, then Aunt weighed down by the rugs and shawls as if under a haystack, then Aunt Luscha and Kirsti each carrying the amazing basket by a handle, then Pappa with suitcases, sticks, umbrellas, rugs and cushions like an overloaded camel. Last of all comes Grandmother and the awful faceless creature leaning on her arm, walking very slowly, as if afraid of falling.

When Njanjan comes indoors, she disappears with the bundle into her own room, and the basket and a number of suitcases and blankets also vanish through her door.

'Don't crowd so, children,' says Aunt Luscha. 'Out of the way, so that Pappa can put the things down.'

'Now you can be really happy,' says Aunt. 'Your little brother has come home.'

'But why hasn't Mamma come?' I ask.

At that moment the door opens and Grandmother and the creature in disguise are standing in the doorway. I press back against the wall and Tommy trips over a suitcase and rushes screaming out of the room.

'Hullo, children,' says the stranger in Mamma's soft, friendly voice. 'How you've grown!'

She undoes the shawls and cloths that had been wound round her head and shoulders – Grandmother helping her – and suddenly it really is Mamma standing in front of us.

But her face is terribly pale and thin and her eyes large and dark. Her face is quite like Mamma's, and yet not really quite the same. When she puts her hand on my head and runs it over my hair, I am not at all pleased with the caress. Although it is infinitely long since she disappeared from here, I know she never spoke or moved in this way, nor did she really look like this. It's another strange Mamma who has come back to us.

'Come, Anni,' says Grandmother. 'You look tired. I've had your bed made up. Leave Mamma alone now, Bernt. She hasn't time for you now.'

At that moment there's a pitiful wail from Njanjan's room, the voice weak and thin, just as if it came from a very small and sad little animal.

'Do you want to come and look?' says Aunt. 'But you mustn't go too close to him, and you must be quite quiet.'

At first I see only Njanjan's back and a lot of clothes flung down on the bed, but then I see a little, wrinkled, dwarflike face inside the bundle of shawls and napkins. It's pink and naked, the eyes tight shut and the mouth wide open and toothless, so the pink gums show under the top lip. Beside the face is a pale little clenched fist. It looks so funny, because it's terribly small and yet is exactly like a real person's hand with fingers and nails and fine wrinkles at the knuckles. Funniest of all is that it moves a little and the fingers bend just like on a real hand.

'Isn't he sweet?' says Aunt.

Njanjan clucks at the bundle just as she does at a squirrel, turning it this way and that, and suddenly he is lying quite naked, kicking at his napkin. His body is almost smaller than his head and consists really of nothing more than a bulging round stomach and a large willie, and the arms and legs are small and crooked with deep, horizontal creases in them. When he whimpers and waves them about in the air, they shake like Aunt Louise's hands. Njanjan lifts him up by the legs and wipes his bottom and thighs, which are bright red. There's a square of bandage in the middle of his stomach, fastened by sticking-plaster, so you can't see his navel – just as if someone had bitten him off there. Every time he whimpers, his stomach arches, the bandage tightens and something grey and wrinkled appears from under it.

'Why has he got that patch on his tummy button?' I ask.

'Because his tummy button hurts,' says Aunt.

'But why does it hurt?'

'All babies have that,' she replies, looking displeased. 'Don't ask so many questions. You shouldn't be inquisitive about such things.'

'But why is he so ugly?'

'He's not at all ugly. I think he's a really sweet and delightful baby, and everyone else says so too.'

'But the babies in the water-lily pool were much more beautiful. Why couldn't we have had one of those?'

'That was just a picture. Everything's beautiful in pictures.'

'But you yourself said all that about the water-lily pool and the stork was true,' I exclaim with disappointment.

'Of course, of course it's true,' says Aunt. 'I just meant. . . .' Then Aunt goes into a long explanation about what is beautiful and what is ugly, about pictures and reality, none of which I understand at all. But she looks worried and now and again stops as if she herself doesn't understand what she is saying.

33

THAT BABY WHICH LIVES IN NJANJAN'S ROOM IS HARDLY EVER seen and you could easily forget he exists at all if you didn't see all those napkins hanging up to dry in the kitchen and Njanjan going into her room with his bottle in her hand.

That bottle which has suddenly come into our house is everywhere and looks so amusing, I often have to stop and look at it. It's a long and narrow bottle with a teat like the red cap of a gnome on top of its head. Sometimes the bottle hasn't been washed and is cloudy, and sometimes it's clean and as transparent as a window-pane. Sometimes it's full of thick, white milk so you can't see through it, and it is cooling in a saucepan of water. The teat is the funniest thing about it because it's like a finger. When Njanjan picks up the bottle and turns it upside-down, the teat looks like a cow's or the nipple on Mamma's breast, and big white drops fall from the tip of it down on to the floor. Njanjan gets awfully angry if you touch it. Her face goes red and she shouts so loudly, it frightens you into running away. The bottle is filled with cow's milk and feeds the baby instead of Mamma doing it, as she's ill and hasn't any milk in her breasts. The baby sucks milk from the bottle every day and is allowed to have it in his mouth as much as he likes, but we're not allowed to touch it, because the teat is the baby's and not ours at all.

Sometimes the baby's basket is put in the living-room or on the closed veranda. But I don't bother to look in it when I go past. Although everyone says I have to like the baby, I don't like it all.

But Tommy doesn't live in Njanjan's room any longer and his bed has been moved into the nursery. Aunt looks after him now, just as she looks after Bernt and me, so suddenly we've become three big boys living with Aunt. Though Tommy isn't all that big. He can't dress or wash himself, and he whines and is awkward about his food. Aunt has to sit beside him and feed him with a spoon. He's always crying and calling for Njanjan, escaping from the nursery and banging on the door of Njanjan's room to try to get in. Aunt has to rush after him, lift him up and carry him back to the nursery again. When she puts him down, he doesn't stay standing up and it's almost as if he'd gone back to being a baby. He falls over on the floor, gasping for breath and tense all over, then howls so that his face turns bright red. No one is allowed to touch him and he kicks and hits out if you go anywhere near him. I'm always afraid he'll burst, because that howl inside him is so great it can't get out.

But sometimes Tommy is almost like a big boy and it's fun that he has moved into the nursery with me. For Bernt often doesn't want to be with me. When he is playing at something and I'm sitting beside him, he says I mustn't disturb him or touch his things, so in the long run it's rather dull just sitting watching. But Tommy always wants to play with me – as soon as I get my toy animals out of the box or tip a chair over to make a ship, he's standing beside me asking me why I am doing that.

When we're playing, he nearly always does what I tell him. If I say we're going to be tigers, then we're both tigers and he leaps around on the floor on all fours just as I do. He extends his claws, yawns so that his whole mouth glows red, and he glances sideways at Bernt, who is crouching in a corner without the slightest idea what huge and dangerous animals have come into the room. When we have wrestled and played for a while and roared so loudly the grown-ups in the dining-room go rigid with terror, we lie down beside each other on the floor, and Tommy purrs and I put my paws round him and lick his untidy, honey-yellow coat so that the hairs lie smooth and gleaming along his body.

But when I get hungry, I don't want Tommy to be a tiger any longer. I tell him he must turn himself into a gazelle so I can eat him up. Tommy turns himself into a gazelle and whizzes like an arrow away through the room. He flies over the chairs and tables, sometimes taking such a desperate leap, his horns hit the lampshade. I race after him. It all goes so quickly, the whole room whirls round. The more excited I become and the louder I pant and growl, the blanker and more frightened Tommy's eyes are when he looks round. And when I have at last cornered him and he can't get away, he curls up in the furthest corner under Aunt's bed, shaking, his shoulders hunched and his nose pressed to the floor like a sacrificial animal about to be slaughtered.

When I hurl myself at him, he lets out a little cry, almost like a cry of joy, or a sigh of relief that the hunt is over and he has at last been captured. When I then sink my teeth into his jugular vein and drink his blood, he laughs quietly and happily, throws back his head and dies with a little panting sigh, as if he felt great relief over never having to be afraid again.

The worst of it is that Tommy can never do anything by himself and so Aunt always has to help him with everything. She hardly has time to look after me. Instead, I make attempts to show how big and clever I have become by trying to manage on my own and turning to her as little as possible, so she will anyhow like me best. She praises me, too, and tells Grandmother and Mamma that I've become such a big boy I can dress myself and do up my front blouse buttons, and I need help only with tying my laces and the buttons at the tops of my stockings and at the back of my trousers and undershirt. But all the same, it does seem rather annoying to be so clever that I have to watch while Tommy stands naked on the edge of the bed in front of Aunt, and she has to hold the pot under his willie when he is going to pee.

AFTERWORD

IN THE SUMMER OF 1941, WHEN VIBORG WAS RECAPTURED AND THE Finnish army advanced to the Karelian isthmus, my company was marching past Teerilä one morning. We were only a few kilometres away from my childhood home. I swung my bicycle into a bumpy side-road leading up to it.

It was good to leave the dusty road full of marching columns, creaking vehicles and swaying gun-carriages. Hitherto, my memories had been of such a distorted nature I scarcely recognized what I saw. My reason told me it was my childhood landscape I was looking at again, but my emotions refused to accept it. It was like seeing a beloved and familiar face distorted by illness.

Everything had been ravaged by the war, an occasional charred tree-stump rising ghostlike against the sky. The bare slopes were all grubbed up, criss-crossed with trenches and tangles of barbed wire. The familiar villas along the road had disappeared, along it now nothing but blackened fire walls and sooty chimneys. One house had burnt to the ground, and inside the stone base was the blackened skeleton of an iron bedstead, a blue enamel can and a cracked chamber-pot staring abandoned up at the sky. A patch of charred grass, a shattered corpse of a horse and the unmoving silhouette of a wrecked tank bore witness to the fighting that had taken place here a few days earlier.

A revoltingly pungent smell reminiscent of funeral wreaths and coffins swept towards me, as if Death himself had breathed on me. The smell lay over the whole landscape and stuck to my clothes, like a perpetual, slightly suffocating sense of anguish deep down inside me. It made the whole area seem nightmarish and unreal. The butterflies fluttering among the flowers and birds twittering in the trees seemed to me to be a delusion, intended to lull me into security and persuade me to forget man's ability to destroy and obliterate life. Only the crows seemed real and at home here. They were swarming over us in thick clouds and their shadows swept like gusts of wind over the road and the fields. Croaking hoarsely, they dived down on to the fields and new clouds kept appearing, as if sucked out of the sky by a vast maelstrom. When the last stragglers, flapping heavily and croaking breathlessly, had disappeared out of sight, all was silent and I could once again hear the deep rumble of guns in the east.

As soon as I turned into the side-road to Teerilä, the landscape changed character, as if I had left the war behind me as I turned my back on the marching columns and headed straight into the safe and peaceful world of childhood. The sun shone and the birds were chattering away, quite untroubled, in the elder-bushes. I dived into the flickering shadows of the pine woods where spiders had strung glittering webs of sunlight between the trees. Here I could find no trace of the war. The forest was as silent and desolate as if no human being had set foot in it for years.

When I was a child, this road was the main road above all others. It was the road to Viborg and the longest road in the world, leading to the great unknown. In parts it now looked more like a dried-up stream, wheel tracks overgrown with grass, here and there the road completely wiped out or hidden by vegetation so that you thought it had come to an end. But my bicycle flew on, purring quietly and contentedly as if burning with excitement to be reunited with the world of childhood.

Then we were flying out of the forest in an abrupt curve, rushing downhill and following the last stretch of road along the edge of the forest. I felt a stab inside me when the familiar silhouettes of the Kuningasvuori, the Kukkarovuori and St Hubertus Mountain slid out behind each other. There was the lake, now almost filled with reeds. Like a river, it followed the road beyond the meadows and now and again allowed a glimpse of its gleaming surface to appear. A warm smell of resin and pine-needles rose from the glade where Grandmother used to rest on her walks. That smell had come to me whenever we returned, tired and hot, from our outings, and it still evoked pleasant images of the homeliness that was soon to envelop me. I caught a glimpse of the stones of my childhood, two gigantic stone faces buried up to their necks in the meadow. There was the pyramid-shaped barn that reminded me of a witch in a grey-patterned, moiré head-cloth, now sagging and on the verge of collapse, the face grown small and shrunken, the eyes squinting with horror. I flew into the avenue where I had run a race with the moon, the friendly rustle of the birches guiding me right to the Black Gate, where nothing was left except a fallen gatepost. Uncle Georg's hill. How ridiculously small, suddenly! The bicycle rushed up it without reducing speed. A moment later, I was up on the mound where our house had been. There was nothing left of it but the stone base, a tangle of nettles and willow-herb grown over it. The flowers threw a pale-violet light over the whole mound, like the last glow from a fire that can no longer compete with the sunlight. The cotton-wastelike seeds left on the willow-herb stems or sailing slowly through the air stuck to my uniform. Remnants of memories seemed to be still hovering around the non-existent house, bumble-bees buzzing dully in the lush foliage as I cautiously made my way ahead. The nettles had spread profusely and it was difficult to avoid getting my hand stung. Before, they had covered only a small area by the kitchen steps and lined one side of the path to the outhouse and rubbish-tip. Now they had crossed the path like a barbaric army, penetrating into my childhood garden and covering the whole of the top of the slope where the stones had once seemed to me to be as high as the Caucasus Mountains. They had even conquered the stone base and the squares inside it – the ground plan of the rooms in which I had lived as a child. I found it difficult to orientate and assign my memories to the right places. Their triangular pagoda-like tops and saw-edged, hairy leaves rose everywhere, their crocodile bite refusing me entry to my memories.

Essentially, I could recognize nothing at all.

The great dark-brown timber house with its dim, shadowy rooms, its outbuildings and balconies, which loomed up above me like a ship whenever I returned there in my imagination, no longer existed. When I looked up, my eyes met nothing but a stretch of blue sky. The mound I was standing on looked astonishingly insignificant. The essence of the picture I was seeing again had been cut away and the vacuum filled with blue colour. The house with its timber walls, its doors, windows and knots in the wood I saw in front of me the moment I closed my eyes, now existed only inside me. My soul had taken on the form of the house and every room enclosed a particular part of my past life.

I suddenly felt someone was watching me. The feeling was so tangible and violent, I put my hand to my holster as I turned round. At first I thought it was a roaming Russian trying to creep up on me, but then I persuaded myself it was all imagination. But as I was still leaning over the nettles and the fluttering, fiery tongues of the willow-herb, I noticed something moving in the undergrowth. Someone was approaching invisibly and soundlessly. I could see the stems bending to one side, then rising again. But there was still no one to be seen – only this wriggling movement in the undergrowth as if a snake were creeping towards me. It couldn't be a Russian, in fact couldn't be anything human, for the plants weren't tall enough to hide him. And yet I was seized with such terror, I slowly retreated from the stone base without taking my eyes off the swaying stems, my hand clenched round the butt of my pistol. Was I seeing ghosts in broad daylight? My nerves were probably in a bad way after the fierce fighting of the last few days. Had this hillock with its invisible house also got its ghosts roaming round the stone base, and was it one of them now approaching?

By now, the invisible creature had reached the stone base. I saw a nettle stem tremble behind the grey granite block, although all other movement had ceased. My heart thumping, I waited. Suddenly – I didn't really see how it happened – just as when a conjuror makes his entrance through a curtain and is suddenly standing there bowing to the audience while the curtain still hides the stage where his tricks are to be carried out – suddenly a black cat with a white patch on its chest and white paws pattered up on to the block of granite, a rather thin and bedraggled cat, but nevertheless it looked dandified and distinguished, rather like one of those come-down-in-the-world old gentlemen who sleep on park benches but wear bowler hats and light-coloured gloves. God knows where the cat had come from or how it had ended up here in the war zone. Presumably it was a Russian cat. Perhaps it was just the place and the atmosphere that reminded me of Murr, the cat we used to pray for when we said our prayers with Grandmother. But in some way it also resembled Uncle Georg.

Clearly the cat was pleased to see me. It blinked ingratiatingly, laid its ears back and miaowed so that the whole of its mouth shone rosy red. Its miaowing sounded pitiable, almost tearful, as if in me it had at last found a friend in whom it could confide its sorrow. Silently, it slid down from the stone base and crept towards me through the grass, miaowing and lamenting all the time. When it reached me, it started circling round my feet, as if drawing magic circles to ensnare me.

Whenever I stepped, it was under my feet, and I had to be careful not to trip over it or step on its paws. It arched its back, its tail thick and stiffly upright. Then it pressed itself trustingly against my boots and lovingly rubbed its cheeks against the dusty leather as if to polish it. Every now and again it lay down and stroked its face against the grass as if the ground itself I had walked on had become worshipful and sacred. When I bent down to stroke it, it arched like a coil to respond to the pressure from my hand. It wound round and round, closed its eyes and stretched out its head with an adoring expression, like someone beside himself with happiness. The glossy black coat ran through my fingers. The tip of its tail curled, the tail wriggled through my hand and again rose above the little pink dot on its backside. Suddenly the cat started to purr – at first low and uncertainly, then stopping as if unsure of my feelings, but more and more contentedly and trustingly. In the end it became one single drawn-out whirring, as if it had a little film projector inside it. Murr's secretive, safe purring could again be heard around me – the happy whirring of my childhood conjuring up images of crackling fires, golden rays of sun and the embroidered cushions in the living-room.

As soon as I let the cat go and got up, it grew anxious and dejected, as if it had realized that time was short and it had to get me to understand something extremely important before I left. To attract my attention, it turned coquettish, striking playfully with its paw at my boot, leaping after my shadow, rushing away and biting a harebell. Although outwardly past its prime, it seemed to be singularly playful and perhaps not even fully grown. It lured me with its tricks over to the garden on the south slope of the hill. A large number of the trees that had once surrounded it had been cut down, and again I was unable to recognize where I was. The sandy path where Grandmother used to walk was quite overgrown with coarse grass. It was hard to see which way it had gone, and what seemed to me in my memory to be a long walk with hundreds of surprises in store had shrunk to twenty or so steps. Then I was on the opposite side of the circle, where the jasmine-bush grew. I used to enjoy pressing my face against the flowers to absorb their strong fragrance until my ears sang and my feet left the ground. The bush was still there, faded and entangled in long, coarse grass, as if sad that no one ever visited it nowadays.

Once when I was very small – it must have been before David was born – my father bought a little tree for each of us and planted them in the garden. I found Tommy's tree at once, a Caucasian pine with soft, tuftlike sprigs. It had grown into a young tree and rose high and slim above the willow-herb and nettles, a conspicuous sign that things here had once looked different. Bernt's silver fir had been considerably taller than Tommy's pine when it was planted, but had never flourished. I searched for a long time for my tree, a dark little spruce with soft needles – they had told me it came from Turkestan – but I couldn't find it. Presumably it had died or been felled.

From the jasmine-bush it was only a few steps down the slope to the other side of the invisible house. This was the way the nursery had faced and a big sallow bush grew there, just behind it the fence I used to crawl under to go with Bernt on his explorations over the meadows. The forest was on the other side, as dark and solemn as before, but strangely enough at a much shorter distance, as if someone had shoved it forward towards the mound on which the house had stood.

The cat had followed me like a shadow and was now sitting beside me in front of the fence, listening with its ears pricked to the soughing from the forest, its yellow eyes sparkling like agates in its black coat. I suddenly realized the waterfall was still roaring over there, as if it had found out I had come back to listen to it. Its tired, melancholy murmur turned into the same wild roar that had kept me awake at night when the nursery window had been open. For a few brief moments I was again the little boy lying in bed listening in wonder to the rise and fall of its roar, coming closer and moving away again, then merging with the ringing of sleep in my ears. Grandmother's face appeared flooded in the evening light, the black lace cap on her head and shadows playing round her eyes and mouth as on a Rembrandt painting. I saw Grandmother calling down the night and plunging the world into sleep, heard her giving orders to the waterfall which would never allow anyone any peace:

'Nur der Bach am Felsen dort
Fliesst und rauschet immer, immerfort.'

A fierce longing for this vanished, enchanted world welled up inside me. I took the cat in my arms, as if by doing so I could retain the past it had evoked for me. I kissed it carefully on its forehead between the transparent amber-yellow eyes. The cat seemed to understand and to be trying to console me, its great solemn eyes glimmering mysteriously, deep down in them the dream gold of my childhood sparkling. I almost heard it whisper 'Do you remember?'

Perhaps it was just saying that with its gaze. For a moment I thought I saw again the rainbow glow round the angel wings, the sparks from the Firebird's feathers and the colours playing in Oliver's magical bubbles. And as if to protect me and not consume me with the magic fire in its look, the cat closed its eyes, thrust its head with a velvety purr under my chin and licked my throat and cheeks. Its whiskers tickled me so that I involuntarily jerked my head back. But then I pressed this secretive creature to me and buried my face in its warm fur so that I could see nothing. Its purring merged with the roar of the waterfall and there was nothing but this soft, safe darkness roaring and thumping in my temples. I wished I had been able to bury myself right in it, to vanish completely inside it and find shelter, as if in a huge embrace.

But suddenly I was frightened. The rumble of guns could be heard in the distance, dull and subdued, like the swirl of drums at the beginning of a symphony. It was war. I was only one among the millions of people whom fate had driven eastwards. For a fleeting moment, the past had appeared to me as it often did nowadays in my dreams. This was nothing but an incident that really had nothing to do with my present life, and I would soon be standing looking over distant, unknown countryside. The cat I was holding in my arms seemed to me suddenly quite alien. What had I really got to do with this stray – was it making up to me just because it was hungry? What had this whole place – which didn't look as I had thought it would, and simply evoked fear and anxiety in me – got to do with me? After all, everything had been so thoroughly destroyed and obliterated, it could never come back again.

Impatiently, I tried to push the cat's paws off from where it had placed them on my shoulders. But it wasn't that easy. It dug its claws into my collar and clung on so hard, its body tensed and arched when I tried to pull it away. I got a nasty scratch on my neck before I succeeded and, when I put it down, it blocked my way. All this affection seemed obtrusive and peculiar.

I didn't want to stay. An anguish – more profound and suffocating than I had experienced in the midst of exploding grenades, machine-gun fire and the screams of the wounded – was increasingly overpowering me, constricting my throat, thumping in my chest and making me start at the sound of my own footsteps. It was so quiet and desolate, I was sure I was the only person for kilometres around. The countryside all round me looked hostile. All this no longer belonged to me but lay beyond the border of my reality, part of an alien, forbidden world. It was high time to try to catch up with my company, which must have gone quite a long way along the main road.

'I haven't time to play with you now,' I said, bending over the cat. 'I've got to go. There's a war on, you know.'

The cat lay quite still as if saying that didn't matter, only the tip of its tail curling impatiently and gracefully, as if wanting me to understand it was expecting something more.

'What do you want?' I said. 'I haven't anything to give you. Look. . . .' I slapped my trouser pockets to confirm my words. 'Empty! I can't take you on the bicycle, anyhow. You'll have to stay here.'

I was feeling more and more ashamed and annoyed. To ease the parting, I reached out and tickled the cat's stomach. Perhaps my impatience made me rather too heavy-handed. At first it was all a game on the cat's part, but after a while it was no longer a game – the cat's ears flattened along its head, its eyes were screwed up and glittering and its back arched into a crescent, then it dug its claws and teeth into my hand so that I swore with pain. It took a moment or so to free my hand from this bundle of biting teeth and scratching claws.

'Bloody cat!' I shouted, looking at the drops of blood welling out of the scratches on the back of my hand. 'Don't you understand that hurts!'

I wanted to kick it, but didn't dare. I fled quickly over the hill to the bicycle I had left in the grass by the roadside. The cat ran after me, miaowing and calling me back, just as if it had all been a joke I had misunderstood. It ran out on to the road as I threw myself on to the bicycle and was still miaowing as the bicycle flew down the ice-cellar slope. The pain in my chest was like the weeping of an abandoned child and made me feel so wretched I didn't dare turn round.